OF
SNOW
AND
SAPPHIRE

THE WEATHER COURT GEM SERIES

KC SILVER

To those learning how to follow their hearts even when the world fights against you.

One

I ce prickled her fingertips, the cold a relief against her snowy skin—a reminder of everything she had to lose. She dragged her cobalt claws against the arm of her frozen chair, an indent forming and disappearing as the ice molded back just as quickly as it melted. The simple touch of her fingers bore insurmountable powers, even now, when most of the land's magic had faded over the past year.

She weathered the meeting with her back straight, as her advisor droned about the housing efforts in the western lands of the Snow Court. Production had come to a stop since the ice started melting. Not surprising news to hear. It had already been seven months since she was crowned Queen Ludelle of the Snow Court. Seven months since her parents had died in that unfortunate accident at sea, and, now, only one month away from her Undertaking.

"All eyes will be on you, Queen Ludelle. You know that during a ruler's first Undertaking, they always decide their consort. Choosing wisely is how the people will know that you care about the wellbeing of this court."

Ludelle lifted her chin, looking down at Balvan, her obnoxious royal advisor who had nothing better to do than pester her about the obvious. "I am well aware of what happens in the Undertaking, Balvan. I do not need you to serve as my reminder."

He tidied up the overwhelming array of papers strewn astray on the table, his delicate hands wizened by time. Balvan always seemed to be carrying those precious sheets with him, like a child and its protective blanket.

"It's actually exactly what I'm meant to do. It's my job to see you succeed," he reminded in a familiar, deadpan tone. "I've been doing this longer than you've breathed."

He was right. At Ludelle's twenty-three, Balvan had decades over her. He'd served as an advisor to her father, and even to her grandmother for a short time after her first advisor stepped down. The Snow Court appreciated his counsel every year by celebrating his labor and guidance, as workers were relieved of their jobs for time to spend with their families. Ludelle thought it a bit much, but she appreciated his help, nonetheless. She had needed it when she'd been so suddenly crowned, but she'd never admit that to him.

"I have been preparing for my Undertaking since I was a child. I am more than ready to take this on." She lied through her teeth. The Undertaking varied for each ruler, so she had no idea what hers would entail. Her father's first Undertaking as King consisted of having to kill a massive snow creature, saving her mother in the process—a joyous occasion, as the people fell in love with her mother's cunning personality. Every year after, her father would go into the woods to vanquish another creature, and in doing so, replenish the Snow Court's powers for the year.

"Are you prepared to finally get married?"

Ludelle ground her teeth. Balvan knew that to be a sore spot for her. She had avoided any advances from nobles her entire life and had refused to entertain the possibility of accepting their hand in marriage. Even though the Undertaking would determine her future betrothed, she still had a choice in the matter. It wasn't about who was on the other side of it, but how willing the ruler was to get to them. It was a test from the Weather Gods to prove how dedicated their ruler was to the court, and how much one was willing to sacrifice to keep the court afloat.

The problem was the expectation from other nobles that she marry one of their own. Every one she faced reeked of dishonesty, disloyalty, and desperation for a seat of power. Fractals began forming on the skin of her palm as she ruminated on the greed of the nobles and the thought of how quickly they would bend a knee to warm her bed—not in the name of adoration but in the pursuit of higher station. That was the sacrifice of her role, she supposed. The burden she must carry.

She shattered the amalgamated ice that had formed around her fingers when she unclenched her hand.

"I will do whatever is necessary to guarantee that our powers do not dwindle; that our court remains strong. Do you doubt me?" she asked, a threat underlying her words.

"Not at all, Your Majesty. You have just been awfully silent about your potential prospects." Ludelle started to protest, but Balvan interrupted her by pointing to one of his hundreds of papers. Truly, how did he manage to keep everything organized? "Here is a list of everyone I deem suitable and everyone I have invited to tomorrow's ball. From there, you will need to narrow it down."

He stormed off, not sparing her a second glance. Taking that as her cue, she exited the council chambers with the list now stuffed into the pocket of her dress, lined with the finest furs. Though her blood ran blue, she still needed the warmth.

Her chambers were at one of the highest wings of the castle—second only to the divine temple room made for direct prayer and connection to the Weather Gods. She weaved through the halls, passing by guards stationed along the walls. She made sure to avoid the games room, knowing that her ladies in waiting would be there, perhaps even a few drinks deep. She didn't have the energy for their mischief today.

"I take it that went well?" A playful voice called out to her. Zimyn leaned against a wall, the cross of his arms accentuating the toned biceps, sheathed by icy scales. All members of her guard were bestowed with this frozen feature and as Captain of the Guard, Zimyn's armor loomed with an iridescent glow; an alluring contrast against his light brown skin. When he first earned them with his new title, he had complained about the pain caused by the sheets of ice entering his skin. He bled, and Ludelle wrapped him up each night until they healed.

"I am in no mood for your antics, Zimyn." She continued on her way, her heels clicking against the frigid floor. She never slipped—a perk of being born in the Snow Court: ice didn't faze her, or any of her people.

She ventured through the long halls, the walls around them plain. Not even a single painting was hung. Just like the ice around them, the castle was cold, with so little life.

She could hear Zimyn following her, so she sped up, hoping to avoid him. Unfortunately for her, his long stride swiftly swallowed the distance.

"Another conversation about your Undertaking?"

"Is it that obvious?" she spat back.

"Well, it is the topic of the season. Everyone is gossiping about it. What horror will the Queen need to face? Who will she marry?" The second question came out more harshly, his light tone turning rigid.

Before she could respond, a figure bounded towards them. Zimyn backed towards the wall, giving Kotyn space. Ludelle's snow leopard circled before bumping her head against the Queen's hand, asking for a scratch. Ludelle gave into her demands. Her soft fur brushed smoothly through her fingers, the movement methodical and calming, and Kotyn nuzzled her head into Ludelle's hands, asking for more. It slowed Ludelle's racing heart. For some reason, just being around Zimyn flustered her, even if they had been friends since childhood.

"My marriage prospects are not your business nor anyone else's for that matter."

He chuckled, then stopped when she shot him a reprimanding look. Stepping closer to her, he bent down so that he was eye level. "Who you choose to marry will forever impact this court. The people have the right to be curious."

Her body became stiff as his warm breath tickled her face. Even crouched down, his tall and wide stature eclipsed her, the closeness of his strength causing heat to pull to her center. They often found each other in these precarious situations, a thread pulling them together before it was snipped. But they could not take that step. At least not yet.

"And if I decide I will not marry at all?"

He brushed back strands of his sky blue hair that teased in whisps over his handsome face. "You know it doesn't work that way." Sympathy oozed from his voice. He understood the pressure of making choices for the sake of others. His father, the former Captain, had happily retired from his station, which meant Zimyn had been expected to take his father's place—and he did it so proudly. "You have traditions to uphold."

She looked into his glacial-blue eyes, the color so unlike her own. Hers were completely white, save for a silver pupil—a royal's eyes, passed down to her. With the responsibility to replenish the court's power permanently branded into her, it served as a lasting reminder every time she looked into the mirror that her people were depending on her.

Zimyn gulped, and she tracked the way his throat bobbed. This was becoming too overwhelming for her. She pulled away before they made a mistake out in the open halls where anyone could see.

"Of course. We must follow tradition," she said, as she smoothed her dress of its wrinkles. "Come Kotyn, it's time for dinner."

Her private chambers offered a view of her Court; the mountainous expanse a comfort to her heart. The peaks in the distance were hers. Homes dotted the land, each filled with lives that were her responsibility. Small snowflakes fluttered, and Ludelle stopped herself from thinking about what would happen if she failed her Undertaking.

Without ice running through her veins, her people would perish because the snow would melt away, and the land would become a giant grave, the mountains without its people.

She couldn't let that happen.

Ludelle had continuous bursts of power throughout the year that she used to sustain the court, but even she had to preserve it as best as possible, as it was a limited resource.

Taking off her crown, one inherited from her grandmother, Ludelle placed it safely on her vanity. The pretty jewels that adorned it stared back at her, but she turned her gaze to herself in the looking glass. Kotyn got comfortable on the Queen's bed, resting on the edge as Ludelle pulled the pins from her hair and shook out the white waves. Kotyn purred, her eyes falling shut without worries. Would it be considered pathetic to be jealous of a large cat?

Unable to rest, Ludelle headed to her study and fished out the list of names that Balvan had given her. As she read through the list of suitable nobles, each name seemed to only be worse than the one before.

Aeden, who hailed from the west, had tried making unseemly advances towards her at every ball. Ludelle ended up slapping him on one occasion, causing a ruckus and a harsh punishment from her mother. Then there was Mitah, who had attempted poisoning Kotyn because he believed that a Queen should not have a pet, instead her sole purpose to produce and care for the future heir. That would never work. Kotyn would eat him in his sleep, while Ludelle gladly watched. Then, Cirrus, of course. The Lord that cared more for his clothing and appearance, than the wellbeing of anyone.

Tomorrow. She would worry about it tomorrow, during the ball.

She crumpled the paper, turned it to ice, and threw it against the impenetrable walls, creating an explosion of fragments, which would just fuse with the castle floors over time—her powers becoming a part of her surroundings.

Ludelle remembered her mother's words, ones spoken only days before her parents had passed. *You are useless without a husband; choose wisely.*

Ludelle tapped her fingers against the desk, growing impatient with everything. She just wanted this all to pass.

"Looks like a bad time," Helena—her cousin—said, as she made her way to Kotyn and smacked a kiss on the big cat's forehead. The beast didn't even twitch.

"What can I do for you?"

Helena pulled off her leather gloves, revealing the same pale skin as Ludelle's, except hers was peppered with small freckles. "I just wanted to check in. Balvan announced the ball to all your ladies in waiting. Liatris actually jumped from her seat in glee."

Ludelle snorted. "Sounds just like her."

Helena stuck her tongue out. "Don't be that way. All of us ladies are just trying to find any source of joy, these days."

Ludelle watched the sun, hidden behind the clouds, go down for the day. "I'm fine." Ludelle finally responded to her cousin's question.

"Do you know who you're picking?" Helena asked hesitantly, as she brushed her fingers through her straight, blonde hair.

"I have an idea."

"Well, as long as it's not Aeden. I heard he went hunting recently and got attacked by a wolf. At least, that's what he claims." Helena inspected her nails, not claws like Ludelle's, but Ludelle knew that Helena sharpened them enough to make sure they could inflict pain. "Witnesses said it was just a large branch that he walked into because he wasn't paying attention."

"It's not Aeden."

"Wonderful," she smiled, as she headed towards Ludelle's closet. "Now the more important question, what will we be wearing?"

11

Helena rifled through her cousin's clothes, throwing gowns on the floor that caught her eye. Ludelle followed her cousin, knowing exactly which dresses would suit them both.

Two

Z imyn stood by the dais, awaiting his Queen's arrival. Guests chatted amongst themselves while a talented musician worked a harp in the far corner. He knew that Ludelle adored the soothing sounds that came from such a grand instrument and taking it in, now, he would have to agree. One day, he hoped to visit the Lightning Court—the place where the player was from. In fact, he itched for the day that he could freely explore the other courts on the continent as a traveler, and not as Ludelle's Captain.

Soon. That day would come soon.

Balvan had wandered in at some point, but Zimyn lost sight of him in the boisterous crowd. He assumed the man was most definitely engaging in political discussions when the ball was supposed to be about Ludelle and her future betrothed. Though he couldn't blame Balvan for taking this opportunity; it was rare that nobles from all corners of the court attended a ball, especially in the last few months when the court was in mourning.

"You look excited," Villeta said. Ludelle's lady in waiting sipped on a glass of sparkling wine with cubes of ice floating in it.

He didn't get a chance to respond before Villeta added, "I heard Queen Ludelle's dress is absolutely stunning."

"Why must I know that?" he asked too sharply.

Villeta's eyes widened. Her voice became sing-songy, like an innocent child. "No reason. Helena just told me, and I thought I would share. With you."

"Why not share with her other ladies in waiting?"

Villeta huffed, her pink colored lips matching her elegant dress. The bright color complemented her tan skin. "Because they're not the ones secretly in love with her."

Zimyn coughed, choking on nothing but air. A few guests shifted their attention onto him, and he flashed them a comforting smile.

"I wouldn't speak so openly about matters you don't understand, Villeta," he chided, his lips downturned.

"Apologies, I just don't understand the charade," she waved him off. "You want each other, yet you refuse to be her consort."

Zimyn sighed. It wasn't that simple. Ludelle could in fact choose him as her consort, but that would not be honoring tradition. Many would look down on her if she picked him because having a noble as her husband would strengthen the court, while choosing a man of his station would weaken her appearance to the realm. It is even said that the more powerful a consort was, the more powers the court would be blessed with from the Weather Gods. The validity of that legend, however, was yet to be determined.

It wasn't that he didn't love Ludelle. He did immensely. His whole life, he did, and leaving her would be like ripping apart his soul. But she needed to pick her consort wisely. Zimyn would then give up his title as Captain as soon as Ludelle completed her first Undertaking. He would be free to travel the continent and she could rule as she had always been destined.

Even though their hearts wanted each other, they both knew—deep down—that their futures conflicted.

Ludelle found herself in the perfect dress to draw the nobles in. It had an a-line skirt made of tulle that had been dusted with glitter, the bodice sheer except for lace snowflakes embroidered on it, and long strands of glitter flowing off her shoulders. The gown was light and perfect for dancing—a skill that had been drilled into her since birth, practically.

Taking one last deep breath, she stepped into the ballroom. The eyes of the crowd all turned towards the Queen, but her eyes only saw him. Zimyn stood with his back stoically straight, the silver of his uniform bringing out the cool tones of his light brown skin and sky blue hair.

She made her way over to the dais, adorned with one icy throne, her dress fanning around her as she sat. This time next week there would be two.

People from all over the court were in attendance, gawking and whispering. They approached to greet her, making small conversation about their lives that Ludelle took great care to remember. Though Ludelle felt like a spectacle, she endured it. She still had so much to prove to her people, and she didn't want to fail them.

Soon the dancing would begin, but for now, she took in the room. This was the last time she would be doing any of this alone. She didn't know if that was a blessing or a curse. Her grandmother told her stories about how people had viewed her differently after her marriage. Not that they lost respect for her, but that conversations turned from ways to improve the lives of the people to questions about when she would bear the heir to the throne. Ludelle worried the same would happen to her; that she would become not a Queen but simply a mother to a future King. She worked too hard for that to become the case, and she would work harder to guarantee it wouldn't happen.

"You look so refined," Helena said, her own navy dress sparkling as she stepped up beside the throne.

"Thank you." Ludelle bowed her head. "I am sure you will catch the eye of someone special tonight."

Helena blushed, sneaking a glance at Villeta. Ludelle's mouth opened slightly. She could pinch herself for being so blind for all these years. No wonder Helena was always quick to rush to Villeta's table during their game nights.

Nobles made their way over to try and persuade her that they were the perfect fit for consort. Some went as far as providing her a detailed plan on how to improve the court. Others came with flowers or jewelry, which she had a guard take them away and give them to the Ladies to rifle through. Bribes wouldn't sway her.

Saira, one of her ladies in waiting who was just a little too nosy, said. "Are you looking for someone?"

"Pardon?"

"You're craning your poor neck so much. Are you seeking out the Captain? He left to survey the perimeters. Apparently there was a giant spill of wine that has now frozen to the castle floor."

"If you must know, I am not looking for Zimyn. I'm merely scoping out the room to decide on my first dance partner."

Saira hummed, but didn't seem convinced. "Let's hope the nobles are better on their feet than you are at lying."

Ludelle snorted, accepting a glass of sparkling wine from a passing servant. The energy of the room grew antsy as she continued sitting on her throne. *Good.* She wanted to build up the tension before she finally let it burst as the music unfolded and the dancing began.

Balvan stepped up to her, bowing cordially in his smart-looking black suit. His face was stiff and his shoulders tense. "It's time to let the festivities begin, Queen Ludelle. The people don't like to be toyed with."

"Are they complaining about drinking quality wine and enjoying the fineness of the castle?"

"Go," he said sternly. So she did, but only after she chugged the fizzy liquid until it burned her throat.

Ludelle stood up straight. The crowd took a collective sigh of relief. "Let the dancing begin," she announced. Her dress glittered

17

around her as she spun, creating an aura of wonder. She spotted Zimyn standing on the far side of the hall, staring at her, like she were the moon pulling in his attention. Then she saw his eyes wander away and a chill swept through her.

The orchestra in the corner began playing a tune of a common waltz, but people still waited until Lord Cirrus bowed and reached out his hand to the Queen. "Can I have this dance?"

Ludelle accepted. They reached the center of the dance floor, and the rest of the crowd stood back to watch them as they gracefully glided across. The noble spun her around, but she had no difficulty keeping up as he guided her through it with such refined skill. His one pale arm on her hip, the other clasping her hand; in truth, she had never felt so elegant than in that moment. Usually she had to push the men in the right direction as they stepped on her toes, but Lord Cirrus had been properly trained—like her.

He wore exactly what she expected a man who came to impress would wear; his royal blue suit was beaded with small diamonds that bit into her skin as he held her close.

Noticing the direction of her eyes, he said, "I have an even larger collection of diamonds at home."

Ludelle had seen the collection on many occasions. Lord Cirrus and his family hailed from the south, where the mines prosperously overflowed with the beautiful rock. It was one of the wealthiest areas of the court, since its stones traded well among the other Weather Courts. Hence, Ludelle had traveled there often with her father and mother for royal business.

"They are beautiful," she said, trailing her fingers along his arms and drawing patterns as she went from one to the next. "Though not as impressive as the revered sapphire."

Each Weather Court had their own gemstone, and the Snow Court's was sapphire; a gift from the Weather Gods that represented abundance.

He chuckled. "Perhaps not, but I do think a diamond has such great depth. Its strength is easily forgotten because of its beauty, but it's tough underneath. Just like you."

Ludelle blushed, but she was grateful when the crowd had now joined the dance floor along with them, creating an atmosphere of delight. Glittering ball gowns twirled around her and laughter rang through her ears.

The first melody strummed to an end, and she was passed to the next noble—Lord Aeden—who was eager but lacked rhythm. Even Balvan took his turn to dance with her as a way to show the people how united they were. If they were in harmony, then the people could trust that the court was in good hands.

Balvan pulled her in and leaned close.

"A wonderful event," he whispered in her ear. It was hard to hear with the music and people all around them celebrating jovially. "Have any of the nobles caught your eye?"

"Yes," she lied. Although she had a duty to pick one of the nobles, none of them actually made her heart sing. Not like Zimyn; but she and him had come to an agreement years ago. She would not pick him as consort. Couldn't.

"And who is the lucky gentleman?"

"That is between me and the Gods."

"Stubborn as always, just like your grandmother," he scoffed lightly. "I hope you chose wisely. All these nobles are a worthy choice."

What made a man worthy? Their riches, power, ability to woo a woman to their bed? No, none of these men felt worthy of her hand. Ludelle thought nobody was—beyond one.

"You know..." Balvan said slowly, solemnly almost. "It'll be a sad day when you have to say goodbye to your Captain. He is such a great asset to the Court, but it's likely for the best that he leaves."

Ludelle narrowed her eyes. He spun her out, and her gaze landed on Zimyn. He stood against the wall, surveying the room.

"What do you mean?" Ludelle asked when she was back in Balvan's arms.

"Captain Zimyn informed me that he was leaving after your Undertaking. He wanted to travel to the other courts. He cannot do that as Captain."

The music around her stalled, or maybe that was just her head going quiet with the dull ringing that had taken over—and she stumbled. Thankfully, Balvan caught her, his hands tight on her waist.

Ludelle didn't understand. That was never what they had agreed to. He...he promised her that he would stand by her side forever. Once she won her first Undertaking and chose a consort, they had agreed to remain lovers behind closed doors.

How could he choose to leave her when the very thought of being separated from him left her heart fractured?

Three

Zimyn considered himself to be a personable Captain, one who his subordinates could comfortably come to with any issues. It was how his father taught him to lead and to build trust amongst the ranks so they listened to his orders and did their jobs with pride. A genuine camaraderie—because without that foundation, the Snow Court would be vulnerable and his Queen would be without a strong unit protecting her.

He could never let anything happen to Ludelle, which is why when the time came for him to leave, he would only give up his title to someone he trusted deeply.

It was the night after the ball, and the guard's quarters—situated on the first level of the castle to be ready in case of attack—always came with a rowdy bunch after dinner. Bellies filled and an over-abundance of drinks consumed. Only a few had to remain on duty during the night, so the rest let loose. And they deserved it. Working at the castle was filled with long days and nights, constantly cautious of everyone, even if nothing had happened to the court in years. His father called it a blessing. Zimyn was more prone to call it luck.

"Hey Captain! Sit down and have a drink with us," Novus yelled out, his own drink sloshing over the frosted glass. Novus was a stiff bastard when on duty, but he knew how to enjoy himself when the occasion called for it. To be fair, Zimyn did, too. Those opportunities were just slimmer since his promotion.

"Not tonight." Zimyn waved them off. He needed to rest. The next month would be full of preparation for the Undertaking, and he had to stay focused.

Like the rest of the court, no one knew what Ludelle would face as Queen. It would all be revealed the day of the Undertaking to her and the rest of the court, meaning Ludelle needed to be ready for anything. Only the minister Sveta was privy to that knowledge, as she served as an agent to the Weather Gods. The information would be brought down to her in a dream. She loved to speak about how she was "the hand that did their bidding"—whatever that meant. Her turquoise eyes shined brighter on the days after the dreams, as if the Gods rewarded her for her work with even more beauty, as if they hadn't already blessed her with such commanding beauty already. Ultimately, people respected Balvan more, since he had political power that directly impacted the court.

"Come on, Zi. You're as tense as a bowstring," Novus said.

"I really shouldn't."

Another one of his guards, Flix, came up from behind him, practically pushing him down into a chair and a cold drink into his hand. It made his mouth water. Not because of the taste, but because of how it could numb his mind.

"I need to speak with you, Flix," Zimyn said as he shoved the drink back to his friend and pointed toward his room. Flix nodded, setting the drink aside, where another guard swiped it up and gulped it down before Zimyn could even blink.

Zimyn's room was nothing special. A bed, a desk, a dresser. His belongings were minimal, but he liked it that way. It would mean less to carry once he started traveling.

He had made the decision to finally leave months ago. Naive, he thought he could handle being Ludelle's secret lover, but as the Undertaking approached and as Balvan pushed her to wed one of the nobles, Zimyn couldn't take it. He would be stepping down.

Flix flopped back onto Zimyn's bed and crossed his arms behind his head. "What can I do for you?"

Zimyn sat down and kicked his feet up on his desk, the icy furniture not even denting under the pressure.

"I have a favor."

"Oh?" Flix straightened. "I hope it comes with lots of ale."

The opposite, Zimyn thought. "It's a promotion. I want you to take over as Captain."

Flix stopped smiling. The blur of alcohol must have worn out. "I'm lost. *You're* Captain already."

"I'm leaving after Lud—Queen Ludelle's Undertaking. I need a replacement."

"Why?"

Zimyn shrugged. "I have my reasons. Ones that I rather keep to myself."

"Then why me?" Flix pushed.

"You've known the Queen as long as me. You two have your own bond, and I know you'll keep her safe."

Zimyn picked up his mother's ring from the drawer of his desk. The silver band was simple, the inside engraved with his name. It was a way to always have him with her, she would say. He always hid it in his room because he was scared of losing it if he carried it on him. But now, he would give it to Ludelle when he left, so she would still always have a piece of him with her.

"I accept."

Zimyn whipped his head up. He expected more of a fight from Flix, but perhaps he understood why Zimyn needed to go; and from the way Flix's eyes caught on the ring, it was evident he did.

"One condition," Flix said. Zimyn quirked one of his brows. "You have a drink with us tonight—to celebrate."

"All right," he relented after a moment's hesitation. "Just this one."

They exited Zimyn's room and the guards cheered when he chugged down his first ale, the bitter liquid sliding smoothly down his throat. Already, he could feel the effects on his brain, the way the world was just a bit fuzzier. For one night, he could forget about responsibility. Forget about Ludelle's white eyes, the way they beckoned him closer—even as they were the very reason he had to leave. And most important of all, forget that he would never be able to be hers.

"Rough night?"

"What?" he barely babbled out, shaking his head in the process as his vision cleared.

"You are turning green." Ludelle said, cutting her poached egg. The yolk ran down her bread, and the sight churned his stomach.

"I slept poorly is all."

Ludelle leaned back in her chair. It was just the two of them in the small private dining room connected to her room, with maids coming in and out to serve her breakfast. Balvan would be joining her later to badger her about her Undertaking again, Zimyn supposed.

"You are not fooling anyone with that lie."

"You want the truth?"

"We have always been honest with each other, Zimyn." Something about her response seemed accusatory, but he continued because they did prefer honesty, even if he was a liar. Guilt coated his stomach at keeping the truth from her, but he knew it was best that she didn't know that he would leave. He couldn't distract her from successfully accomplishing her Undertaking with such an admission.

"I lost a game of cards to my guards. My losing hand earned me a chug of five drinks in under five minutes." It had taken all his effort to not vomit the contents back up. Waking up this morning had been even harder.

"Ah. A very proper way to spend the night, I am sure."

He rubbed his temple. "Proper would not be the way I'd put it."

"And if the castle had been attacked?" she challenged. "How would my drunk Captain of the Guard protect me then?"

He knew it to be a joke, a taunt. They played with each other that way. Throwing their position at each other, a way to tease each other. Zimyn also guessed they used it to keep each other in line. Today, her teasing didn't hit the same.

"We haven't been attacked in centuries."

"Not the point," she shot back as she stabbed her fork tongs through a piece of sausage.

If she wanted to play, then he could, too. He stepped away from his station at the dining room door and walked closer, one foot in front of the other, not a blip off balance. "Then I would splash some cold water on my face and drag myself to you no matter how much my body fought against it." His voice lowered, turning rougher. "I'd cut down anyone in my way, ripping each icy scale off my body and throwing them at the enemy until I was just flesh, again, to save you. I'd show everyone in my path exactly why I earned the title of your Captain of the Guard. Then I'd have you freeze their blood as trophies so it would serve as a reminder to everyone roaming these halls of what *we* are capable of."

He was now directly on the opposite side of the table, his hands pressing hard into the metal, the cold biting his skin. Ludelle stared him down. Even though she was sitting and he was standing, she still held dominance. A true Queen holding court. Except for the tinge of blue blush on her face.

"Good," she said simply, going back to her breakfast, but he could tell that his words had rattled her. He meant every syllable. He would fight to the death to ensure her safety. She was his to protect, and no marriage, no distance between them, would ever change that. He would always have ears on the inside of the castle ensuring it.

"Glad we could clear that up."

"I take it you're too tired for our training today, then?"

He laughed. "Now you're just looking for excuses. I am perfectly capable of commanding you around for an hour."

She grumbled, but didn't let her annoyance show any further. Ludelle hated training with him just as much as she hated having to choose a husband. Every time she prayed to the Weather Gods, she informed him that she begged for a challenge of the mind as her Undertaking instead of a physical one.

He hoped it, too. That's where her strengths were. She could run circles around others in any mental game, but a fight of strength would be her doom if she didn't train for it. Hence the almost-daily training with him. She needed to be equipped to use any weapon: her fists, her surroundings, and anything in between.

She had improved greatly in the years that he'd taken her under his wing, but one could never be over-prepared in these matters. So he pushed her and she let him because she understood the importance of it.

"You have always liked being in control," she said, her tone turning sultry. Or maybe he was just imagining it, the alcohol still in his head, but the way her eyes had narrowed and honed in on his body made it tighten. "Bossing people around."

"It makes me good at my job," he choked out, trying to calm his racing heart.

She hummed. "But what will people think of me when they hear that you ordered around a Queen?"

"The people wouldn't believe it."

"Oh?" Her brow arched.

He wouldn't say it, even if she was goading him. The court knew that she had him wrapped around her sharp fingers, those claws latched onto him years ago. Rumors spread about how deep their relationship ran. He worked overtime to quell them, but Ludelle wasn't oblivious.

"You should finish your breakfast." He cleared his throat. They needed to end this before they went too far. "Balvan is waiting for you."

He could have sworn her shoulders deflated a bit, but she quickly recovered, her disappointment gone in a flash. Her lips tightened and back straightened, her cold front back on.

He opened the door for her, and she didn't hesitate as she passed through, but the smell of winter honeysuckle and pine lingered in her absence.

Four

"You must be excited," Liatris said cheerily. Her pale skin, though not as white as Ludelle's, turned flush with glee. Kotyn shook awake from her spot near the window, yawning and showing her sharp teeth in protest of the disturbance to her slumber. Ludelle liked to think that Kotyn learned that maneuver from her.

"Excited for what, Liatris?" Ludelle put her book down, one that she had hoped to read in silence, but Balvan insisted that she spend some time with her ladies in waiting, explaining that another woman's opinion might help her make her decision on which suitor would be worthy of her choice. Ludelle had to restrain herself from leaping on top of the man and blasting ice down his throat until he choked and died. Why did everyone else's opinion matter more than her own? She was Queen after all, shouldn't people come to *her* for counsel?

Plus the mixture of perfumes in the room did the opposite of what Balvan hoped. Her head throbbed everytime she had to breathe in the abstract aroma of a perfume imported from another court.

More cautiously now, Liatris responded, "Well...marriage of course. It's such a joyous occasion."

The other ladies nodded their heads enthusiastically, trying to be encouraging but Ludelle knew they had their own motives. Ladies in waiting could not marry until the Queen was wed. They could not bear children until Ludelle did, too. It was an outdated custom that Ludelle wanted cut from the law, but she could not make changes before her first Undertaking. She needed to first prove herself to the Snow Court—which was fair, but frustrating.

"Yes, of course." She sipped on her tea, her book now long forgotten, and the room seemed to relax. "My marriage will be filled with wondrous joy. A man will come into my life, claim his title as my consort, and spend the rest of his days trapped in a dungeon cell."

One of the ladies dropped her spoon, the sound clattering loudly. A maid rushed over to pick it up and another offered a fresh spoon. Saira sheepishly accepted it.

"Pardon?" Villeta exclaimed in horror, her brown eyes blown wide.

These women were too easy to frighten. Too bad she didn't have a choice in picking her ladies in waiting, either. She would have preferred a bunch who were a bit more bloodthirsty. Even her cousin Helena was much too sweet-natured for Ludelle. Though at least she didn't walk around Ludelle like the ice of the castle floor was melting.

Helena currently sat next to Villeta on a plain white chaise, her hands on her lap. Helena's deep purple gown couldn't hide Villeta's own hands which inched closer to her cousin's. Ludelle took note to offer them support when they were finally free to marry after Ludelle's own nuptials. Now was not the time to bring it up.

"I jest, ladies." Ludelle smiled sincerely, even showing her teeth. "He will live comfortably, warm my bed, and once I have an heir, he will be fed to Kotyn." The silence became palpable and awkward. Ludelle had to stop herself from rolling her eyes at their seriousness. "Truly, this is just me making light of a difficult situation. I am nervous about my first Undertaking. I'm sure you understand?"

"Of course," the ladies echoed.

"I have been told I need to ask for your help on who I should choose as a husband." Since they didn't want to entertain her honest thoughts, they would move on to a truly grim topic.

Thankfully, that lit up the room again. Each of them stated their opinions before Ludelle could even mention that she had narrowed down the nobles to four options this morning, before meeting with Balvan. He had been pleased with her remaining selection. That made her want to reconsider her options. Surely, they couldn't have the same taste. Though she did notice his jaw clench when he got to the last name: Lord Cirrus. Ludelle wished he was only there for spite, but Ludelle truly believed he was the best of the bunch.

"Well, it can't be Lord Trevan. I heard he has an affinity for walking naked around his home," Villeta said.

"That doesn't sound too bad," Helena giggled, covering her mouth like a proper lady. Ludelle's mother always liked to compare the two of them when growing up. She believed that Helena had the right composure and manners for Queenhood, while Ludelle was too wild. There wasn't even a point to her mother's opinion since Helena was not destined to be Queen, unless Ludelle died without an heir. Then, the Weather Gods, specifically the Goddess of Snow, Moroza, *might* bestow the honor to Helena. Ultimately, her mother was being cruel only to get into Ludelle's head and make her feel unworthy of a title that was hers from birth.

Villeta said into her tea, as if knowing her words were too vulgar for such a refined setting, "Well, when you live in the Snow Court, it doesn't flatter his cock."

"I heard it shrivels up," Helena added. If only her mother could see the lack of her propriety, now. Villeta leaned her head onto Helena's shoulders, a blush staining her cheeks. Ludelle truly wondered how she could have been so blind to their clear adoration of each other.

The rest of the room snorted. Ludelle scratched behind her ear, trying her best to put on a smile.

"And who has caught your eye, Queen Ludelle?" Saira asked.

Ludelle looked at the closed door, knowing who waited right outside it.

"Captain Zimyn is handsome," Liatris said with a sigh, as if she was dreaming of him.

"I never said such a thing," Ludelle snapped.

"We don't need words to know where your mind wandered." Villeta teased, her tone increasing in pitch.

Ludelle tightened her lips, unable to have this conversation. Her heart physically hurt because of what she recently learned. Zimyn planned to leave her. Everything they had planned and dreamed would be crushed.

Helena jumped in. "Maybe we should talk about the latest fashion instead."

Ludelle gave her cousin a grateful look, as the ladies quickly changed the subject to the growing trend of leather cloaks. Ludelle participated where she could, but even the switch in topic could not dissuade her mind from thinking of Zimyn. Once she completed her Undertaking, he would be gone. Any potential of them being together would be officially severed. They were on two different planes, now, and her marriage would only separate them further.

Ludelle hated the training rings. Not the actual act of training. The movement required was a reprieve from reading official court documents all day. She hated that the guards had no qualms giving their unsolicited feedback about her improper form, or the way she scrunched her face to focus, even if their advice was always helpful.

Growing up, Ludelle had practically begged Zimyn to train her somewhere privately, but he refused, saying that as Queen she should be comfortable sharing space with her subordinates. It was a humbling experience to say the least.

As a compromise, they always worked in an isolated corner, still visible for all to see but at least she wasn't in the center like some kind of common street performer.

"You're distracted," Zimyn said from his place along the wall, a sword in hand that he polished with a rag. He had received that sword as a gift from her parents when he was given the title of Captain and he treated it with great honor. Ludelle found it endearing on most days, but not now.

"Am not," she shot back, shaking her shoulders out to loosen her body, which had become more tense with each passing day.

"You've been standing there for ten minutes and haven't thrown a single dagger."

"I'm warming up."

"We live in the Snow Court. There's no such thing."

She gave him the middle finger, unpleased with his horrible humor. Not wanting to give him another reason to make another joke, she threw a small dagger at the target. It hit off-center to the outermost ring on the right side.

Zimyn raised his brows. She tried again, once more hitting off-center. She cursed under her breath, throwing another hastily in anger, which completely missed and clanged to the floor. She could feel the eyes of other guards on her now, their own training paused and intrigue piqued. She took a deep breath and didn't allow herself to make a scene.

"Let's hope if you face anyone in the Undertaking that they show mercy on you and purposefully run in front of the knives."

"And you can do better?" A stupid question that she regretted as soon as it left her mouth. He knew it, too.

"Is that a challenge?"

"No."

He shrugged, sheathing his sword and slowly stretching his arms as he made his way over, his scales shining in the afternoon light. He extended his hand, and Ludelle placed a knife into it. Their hands barely brushed, yet a shock of desire sparked through her.

Without even sparing the target a glance, keeping his attention zeroed on Ludelle, he threw the dagger. Neither of them broke eye contact as the room around them blurred into a blue haze. His musky pine scent filled her nostrils while his icy blue eyes captivated her. All of it was so consuming that she forgot what they were even doing.

Her body inched forward, a pull that she couldn't resist. Why did they always find themselves in these scalding situations?

"Bullseye," he whispered in her ear. Being a foot taller than her, he needed to bend down considerably.

"You didn't even look."

"I didn't need to look. I always hit the target." He shrugged. "I'm just that good."

"Too bad all that skill will go to waste," she muttered, now focusing on the target instead of him. Beside her, he stiffened.

"What does that mean?"

"It means..."

Someone cleared their throat. "I didn't realize training required exchanging secrets."

Both of them stepped quickly away from the other. A blast of cold ran through her with Zimyn no longer near. The rest of the room was pointedly not paying attention to them. Grunts and slashes of swords echoed in the room, but Balvan stood expectantly behind them, expression grim.

"You have an early morning tomorrow, Queen Ludelle," Balvan said. "It would be in your best interest to get an early rest."

She nodded, still trying to get her bearings again. Zimyn had started cleaning up the area, aggressively removing the daggers from the target and putting them away. He didn't look her way again. She wanted to reach out to him, to take his strong hands in hers, and show him exactly where he should be aiming. But such unproductive thoughts would get her nowhere.

In fact, she needed to stop allowing herself to even think of his hands on her. It would never be. She would never get to experience his weight over hers as he thrusted into her, never feel his hot mouth on her core. Worst of all, he would no longer be hers to command.

She headed toward the exit, her fighting leathers chafing her bristling skin. She couldn't wait to get the blasted things off. "Thank you for your concern, Balvan, but I can take care of myself."

Balvan led her out towards the courtyard—giving them privacy—as he said, "Can you? You two were breaths away from ruining everything. Who will want to marry you once you've sullied yourself with a low born, like him?"

"Who would not want to marry the Queen?" she challenged.

"You think you have more power than you do, but until you have shown the people that you can replenish the Court, you are nothing more than a caged animal being watched." He glared back through the archway at Zimyn, who was still distracting himself with the equipment. "This childhood crush cannot be your future. "

"Where are you taking me?" Ludelle whispered in the quiet night, her parents and grandmother asleep already and only a few guards scattered the premises.

"It's a surprise," Zimyn had said with an airiness to his voice.

They had snuck out of the castle together. He had his hands in hers as he guided her outside somewhere, but he refused to tell her where, which deeply annoyed her.

She should have been entertaining Lord Mitah who had visited with his mother. Ludelle found him to be boring. He lost a game of cards with her, and instead of being impressed and congratulating her, he threw a fit. His pride was wounded, Ludelle supposed. She mentally crossed him off the list of potential future husbands for when that time came. Not for many years, she reminded herself.

"Are we almost there?" Ludelle whined. Her feet were starting to tire.

"*Almost,*" *Zimyn reassured her. His hand touched the small of her back and guided her in front of him.*

Father's Undertaking had just been completed a few days ago, and she could smell the oncoming blizzard. She couldn't wait to see the lands covered in snow, especially the village right by the castle. She would need to go down there. The village—the whole court actually—came alive during the first snowfall after the Undertaking. She thought fondly about her favorite tree syrup treat created with the first snowfall; the villagers would pour the golden liquid onto the cold snow, creating a delicious delicacy.

"Open your eyes."

Ludelle did, and her vision needed a moment to adjust. At first, she didn't know what she should be looking at. They were in the middle of the forest, but there was nothing special. Then, she heard a tiny mew echo up from her feet.

A baby snow leopard inched towards her. It looked hesitant and scared.

"Wh-what is this?"

Zimyn chuckled at her shock. "A snow leopard, Ludelle. I found her a few days ago."

"Where's her mother?"

Zimyn's face became solemn as he crouched down and allowed the small animal to come to him. The cat sniffed his hand. "We don't know. I've been feeding her everyday and she's been alone each time."

Ludelle bent down, her midnight blue cloak getting caught in the twigs and bramble, but she didn't care. The tiny kitten came to inspect her wearily. Ludelle created a small icicle from her fingers, and the kitten licked at it with its prickly pink tongue.

"She's so sweet. Does she have a name?"

Zimyn was breaking up a twig into small pieces. "I've been calling her Kotyn."

"Kotyn?" Ludelle asked. "You named it after Moroza's cat?" As Zimyn nodded sheepishly, Ludelle added. "I like it."

"I thought she could be yours."

Ludelle lost her balance slightly, causing the animal to back away. "Mine? My parents would hate her. I couldn't subject her to that."

"Well, I think she needs a home. At least until she's older," he added. "I also think she needs companionship. Someone who will be by her side. Just like you have me."

Ludelle looked at Zimyn, then—really looked at him. His sky blue hair blew in the breeze, and his eyes shone brightly, like two moons calling to her.

"You'll always have me," he rasped.

Ludelle's gut tightened. Because yes, he would always be there as her Captain, but she wanted something more. He did, too. They always did.

Ludelle picked Kotyn up and pulled her into her lap as she sat down on the cold dirt.

"Would you be by my side as a husband?"

"No," he shook his head. It hurt for her to hear it, even if she knew that would be the answer. "I don't want that pressure and all those eyes on me."

"I want to change this court," Ludelle said quietly.

Zimyn nodded. He understood her desires more than anyone. Whenever they found themselves alone, she would whisper of all the changes she would make as Queen. How she wanted to start a council of representatives from each region of the court, how she wanted ladies in waiting to have more freedoms to make choices for themselves, how she wanted her own children to be able to choose a consort of love. No more pressure of choosing a powerful noble who would be advantageous to the court.

"But I still want you."

Zimyn gulped, "Me too."

But what they wanted were so at odds with what the court expected.

"Then have me secretly," Ludelle said. "Have me wholly behind closed doors where eyes cannot see."

"That...that sounds like a bad idea."

Kotyn fussed in her hands so she let her go. Kotyn wandered the small area, sniffing the leaves but keeping close by.

"Once I have you," Zimyn said. "I don't think I'll ever be able to let you go."

Ludelle sat back on her hands, letting the dirt soil her hands and the sticks bite into her pale skin.

"Then we wait," she suggested. "I'll complete my first Undertaking, marry my consort, and then we can be lovers in secret."

Zimyn considered her words, rubbing his chin. "It might take years, decades even, before you need to do your Undertaking."

"I will wait as long as it takes to finally call you mine. Any amount of time together will be enough."

"I love you, Ludelle." He said it so easily, so simply, and her heart fluttered. *"I would wait centuries to have you, even if our time together is only seconds. I would find you in another life, just to have you again."* Zimyn gently kissed her lips, offering only a taste of what she one day hoped to have in full.

Five

The carriage ride had been bumpy and uncomfortable—not because of the constant bouncing that caused her to hit her head against the velvet interior, but because of Balvan's nonstop briefing, as if she knew nothing of her court. Ludelle had spent her whole life studying the court's politics, history, and economics. She was well aware of the importance of the west's need to maintain ice production in order to preserve meat for the year. The way Balvan spoke, though, one would think she had never even heard of the Snow Court before. It was insulting.

It didn't help when at each village they passed, there was a line of people watching the carriage wheel through the streets. Ludelle waved at them, but they had their arms crossed and their eyes downcast. She couldn't blame them; their lives depended on her, and she had yet to prove herself. Balvan had prepared her for the cold hard truth of the people's uncertainty.

"They expect you to instill confidence. That you will pick a powerful match and maintain the stronghold of the Snow Court," Balvan said obnoxiously, his nasally voice grating more than usual today. At least he strategically wore browns and blacks so she could contrast nicely in her white gown. He knew that optics were just as important as actual political dealings. "There cannot be even a hint of any doubt coming from you, so you will let them know that you have chosen your husband already."

"And if they ask who I have chosen?"

"You're Queen. Tell them it's not their business."

"I do not think avoiding answering a simple question will instill confidence in the people."

Balvan's jaw tightened, unimpressed with her opinions and her quick dismissal of his advice. "Then tell them it will be a surprise. That you want your last few days before your marriage is officially announced to be one of private companionship."

The word companionship rankled, but she swallowed down the bitterness of it.

"So that they can spread more rumors about who sleeps in my bed?" She snorted. "Nothing about my life is private."

He adjusted his long coat. "Well it's better than people gossiping about that brute and you running away together."

She tsked. "Now, that is not very becoming of you. That brute has been key to my training for the Undertaking. He has made me stronger and more prepared." Ludelle didn't even know why she was defending him, why it even mattered anymore. Zimyn would no longer be Balvan's concern. Much less her own.

Ludelle continued, as she tapped her cobalt claws against the frosted window. "Your lack of confidence in me makes me question my abilities. Maybe it's time to reconsider what you add to the court."

He smiled, a silver tooth peeking through. Although years older than her—the same age her grandmother would be if she still lived—he was still handsome. His long brown hair, expertly done, and his clothes perfectly pressed. "You would't dare. The court loves me and trusts me. They have for a long time. And your grandmother would turn in her grave if she knew you had relieved me of my position."

"Now, I see where all that confidence is," Ludelle retorted, as she uncrossed her ankles to take up more room in the tight space. "You have none to bestow unto me because it is puffed up in your mind. Is that why you look like your head is seconds away from popping off your neck?"

"I don't know who you think you are—"

"The Queen," she interjected plainly.

"But you are nothing without me. This court would have long melted to a flood zone weren't for me."

"We will see."

Ludelle stood atop a hill. Ominous gray clouds stretched across the sky, yet there was no snowfall to be seen. The Weather Gods mocked her. Since this village was on the outskirts of the court, furthest from the castle, they experienced the effects of dwindling powers first. The castle that stood at the center of the court brimmed with the final drops until the day of the Undertaking.

This brought Ludelle and Balvan here, still miles away from their intended destination. The rest of the way to the western village needed to be trekked on foot as the roads were beginning to soften, and the wheels of the carriage would have gotten stuck in the mud. Her guards flanked her, now, in case of an attack, but the quiet rural village didn't pose a threat. Zimyn stayed to the back, ensuring nothing went awry from behind them. He avoided her gaze, just like she avoided his.

"We're doing our best to keep everything in order," the villager said. He had greeted them when she had arrived and introduced himself as the head of the hunting groups, as this area was the meat capital of the court with their forests bountiful with deer, rabbits, and wolves. Meat farmers bred cattle, which was the largest source of protein. The weather conditions made it hard to grow any produce, so the court relied on trading the meat with other courts like Rain and Sun for it.

This was not the welcoming party that she was used to, but the sight in front of her explained why.

"As you can see, we're struggling," the villager said.

Struggle was a light way of putting it. The roads had flooded over, the snow and ice all melted. Ludelle, in her warm cloak, was beginning to sweat. The Snow Court desperately longed for the

Undertaking to happen soon—more added pressure to her already growing arsenal of it.

Right as she planned to turn back and address the villager, a child ran out of her home, catching Ludelle's attention. A long braid that hung past her knees fluttered behind her as she slid across the mud, falling and laughing. This child had no concept of the terrible source of her fun; obliviousness could be a freedom—one Ludelle never allowed herself to dream of, because that would be selfish of her. How could she complain when her life was full of luxury and privilege?

The little girl wiped her face and rubbed mud all over it, but she didn't appear upset, moreso just in awe of the changes to her world. The child's mother called out from the stoop of their cottage, and the little girl obeyed orders as she slumped her way back inside.

Sighing, Ludelle said, "I do not understand. I have never seen it get this bad."

She had visited villages days before her father's Undertakings many times. And yes, the snow had dwindled to almost nothing, but frosty patches remained. The people were able to comfortably withstand it.

But this...this was another story. It practically looked like the Rain Court at this point, with patches of puddles and water dripping off of leaves.

The villager sucked on his lower lip, thinking to himself. "We've theorized it's because it's your first Undertaking. The Weather Gods are truly testing you and reminding you of what can happen, especially if you do not choose wisely when it comes to your betrothed."

Of course. The Weather Gods *would* do this. Wedge a boulder in her brain until it knocked sense into her. Too much rode on her shoulders—she needed to get her act together. No more dawdling and stalling. No more brooding about Zimyn's departure. She took a labored breath, her energy waning. She could see from her peripheral that Zimyn shifted on his feet as if noticing it, too.

Her advisor remained silent, letting her take the lead. Although he could be a pain in her ass, he did know how to wield his strengths to allow her to shine. He stepped in when necessary but allowed her to do her job.

"We only have a few weeks left before this will be solved," Ludelle said. "We need to transport all the meat to another village for the time being to make sure it does not rot. Somewhere more central, ideally."

The villager nodded, taking note as she continued. "We'll provide a carriage that will be filled with ice so it stays cold during the trip. In the meantime, I'll be praying to the Weather Gods for a flurry of snow."

"Thank you, Your Majesty," the villager said with deference as he bowed. "We are most grateful for your care. Whichever noble wins your hand will be a lucky man."

She wanted to yell at him to stop because his obvious appreciation for her as his Queen was just another reason as to why she couldn't let her people down. She loved her people but hated facing the reality of how much they leaned on her. It made every decision harder, every desperate urge to damn the consequences and choose the love of her life impossible.

Balvan gave her an impressed look as if he too knew where her mind went, proving how correct his insistence to let Zimyn go was. Responsibility to her court would always come first, and now she couldn't convince herself out of it, even at the expense of her heart.

Zimyn left the traveling party to step into the small town at the center of the village. He left Flix in charge of ensuring everyone's safety as another "test to practice his skills as soon-to-be appointed Captain," Zimyn told him. Flix jokingly saluted him and went to do his job.

The town was sparse in comparison to the one near the castle, but it still had its charm. Many people seemed to be staying indoors to avoid the slick, mud covered roads. Zimyn, himself, had slipped a few times, needing to grab the nearest fence or tree to stay upwards. He spared his horse from traversing through these roads, let the poor animal rest with the entourage of guards.

He stepped inside a butcher shop, a smoky scent overwhelming his nose immediately. He greeted the owner, taking a close look at the freshest cuts. Most of what he sold was from the cattle farms, as the deer and rabbit meat was generally kept for the castle or for trade since it was more expensive.

Zimyn picked a sausage for himself and ate it as he walked around some more.

In a few weeks, he would have the luxury to do this everyday. He could explore every corner of every court. He had the rest of his life to do it, and there would be no limits. He would say yes to every opportunity presented to him. A perfect distraction from the woman with white eyes whom he loved.

His next stop—the real reason he left the group—was the leather shop. He needed some sturdy boots for himself.

"Ouch!" the shop owner yelped. She hit her head on a shelf as she stood up at the sound of his entrance.

She was probably unused to visitors. He didn't think that many of these villagers could afford quality leather like what she offered. Most of the fine leather was traded to other courts or sold to the rare traveler who passed by.

"How can I help you?" she asked.

He pointed to his feet. "New boots."

She nodded and guided him to the back. "We have a few already made," she said. "But I think you might need to be sized for a custom pair."

Zimyn had expected that. The owner sat him down and started measuring his feet. He sat there watching her, the skill and craft and care she placed into her work. Something that seemed so simple on the outside, yet so essential to everyday life.

"Such large feet," she commented under her breath.

Zimyn huffed. She wasn't wrong. When he was young, there was a point where he didn't grow taller, but his feet grew bigger. Thankfully, over time, his height matched the feet that carried him, but it was an awkward few years.

Once the woman finished, she took his name and let him know when it would be ready.

He left the shop feeling such relief and excitement. The time was coming.

There was a small step right by the door of the shop that he forgot about and his foot landed on wet mud, causing him to fall straight down.

"Hopeless," a familiar voice muttered.

Zimyn scrambled up, his uniform covered in mud. Ludelle was standing there, smirking at him.

"What are you doing here?" His eyes darted around. "What are you doing here *alone*?" he asked, more alarmed.

"I could ask the same," she said inspecting her claws. He always loved the way the natural cobalt contrasted with her white skin.

"You should be with the others. You look like you couldn't even fight away a small rabbit if it attacked you."

Her mouth gaped. "What does that mean?"

"It means you look tired."

"I'm fine." But her jaw tensed. She knew he was right. He noticed it while they were speaking to the villagers. It was subtle, but he could see how hard she worked to keep her eyes open. He couldn't blame her. She was under immense stress.

He reached out his hand. "Come on," he said. "Let's get you back to the castle."

She reluctantly took it. Her hands were cold in his, so he squeezed tight, like he could infuse his own strength into her.

"You never said why you were in that shop."

"It's not important."

He could have sworn he felt her heartbeat stop for just a moment, but he didn't push it. He would tell her the truth soon, no matter how hard it would be.

As she promised the villagers, Ludelle went to the quiet divine temple room. The room was situated under the highest peak of the castle, as it reached closest to the Gods. Sveta had unlocked the room for her but gave her the privacy Ludelle craved. Being Queen meant that someone was always seeking her out or trailing in her shadow. However, she used her prayer time as an excuse to get people away because no one dared interrupt her as she spoke with the Weather Gods.

But all good things must come to an end, so she ended her session with one final ask to the Gods that her Undertaking be successful and blew the cold blue flames of the candles out.

The minister waited for her in robes so deeply blue they were practically black.

"May the Weather Gods hear your prayers," Sveta said softly.

"Yes, let us hope that they took time out of their very busy lives to listen."

"Do not forget that we are at their will. Everything we do must serve them."

Ludelle scoffed. "And why do they not serve us?" Especially when Ludelle's family had to risk their lives each year just to please them.

Sveta looked out the large window in the hallway. Small birds chirped as they fluttered around the trees. "They give us the power to live."

"Is it really living when one has such minimal say in how they can live it?"

"You speak of your marriage, don't you?"

"No."

Sveta smiled, dipping her head as if sharing a joke with the Gods personally. "You must make sacrifices, as we all do."

"Surely a marriage of love is more powerful than one that is forced due to responsibility."

"A very astute thought, my Queen. One that I myself have pondered." Sveta tapped her fingers against the small prayer book in her hands, her brown skin blending in with the brown leather. "Ultimately, the Undertaking is a way to prove to the Gods that you are willing to do whatever it takes to protect your court."

A weak response, but Ludelle needed to move on to a different topic. A more urgent one.

"Power is depleting faster than normal. The western villages are practically under water with how quickly the snow and ice is melting."

"That is strange." Sveta rubbed her chin. "It could be a sign."

"Of what?"

She shrugged. "It's hard to know for sure. Perhaps that your Undertaking will go poorly, that you'll fail."

"How encouraging," Ludelle said with a straight face but a spur of concern caught in her chest. She couldn't let that happen.

"I am only here to listen to what the Gods tell me. If you seek comfort, then I'm sure one of your ladies in waiting will gladly provide it."

Ludelle could always count on Sveta to bring the Gods into everything.

"My powers are also causing me trouble."

That piqued Sveta's interest. "What do you mean?"

"I have noticed that I am tired more often." Ludelle put her palms upwards, creating a small flurry of snow. She winced as she did. "And something as simple as that physically hurts."

"It's not unheard of for the royal to struggle with their powers before an Undertaking. I wouldn't worry too much. You won't have them to use during the Undertaking, anyways." She gave Ludelle a gentle pat on her shoulder. "Get some rest. Long days are ahead of you."

Six

With Ludelle off doing her prayers, Zimyn had spare time to visit his father—something that became rarer once Ludelle had been crowned. His responsibilities had escalated, his time diminished, especially with the Queen's Undertaking close at hand. A part of Zimyn felt guilty for not spending more time with his father—especially after his mother had died—but his father understood the role of Captain better than anyone else, so he knew what it entailed: how much time and effort it required to guarantee that his guards stayed in line and that Ludelle didn't find herself in any precarious situations.

Plus, Zimyn didn't appreciate his father's sly glances whenever Ludelle's name was mentioned. For some reason, his father got it in his head that Zimyn's affection for her went beyond the role of her Captain. To be fair, he wasn't wrong, but he still didn't need to constantly throw it in Zimyn's face.

His father lived near the castle, an honor given to him for his years of hard work. Zimyn trekked down the mountain on foot, zig zagging through the dense woods used as an extra layer of protection. With snowfalls becoming more sparse and the weather turning warm, the ground had turned to mud. The steep decline forced him to grab on to the nearby trees. Moss coated his hands.

He often had to stay inside the castle walls, not given the chance to be out unless he accompanied his Queen, which had become slimmer since Balvan had worked hard to keep them apart in public. Hence on those occasions that he did travel with Ludelle, they now acted as if they were strangers, instead of two people who'd known each other since childhood.

"My son," a rough voice spoke out. "You have returned."

Zimyn had to restrain himself from rolling his eyes as he closed the cottage door and stepped inside. "Don't be dramatic, Father. I didn't leave in the middle of the night without a word. You know exactly where I am."

"Can a father not miss his only son?"

"Not when the son has been busy taking over his father's duties so that he could relax without a worry in the world." Zimyn put his hands on his hips. He was careful to avoid the fur rugs dispersed across the floors to protect against dirtying them with his shoes. "What are you doing?"

His father was seated on an old wooden chair, which creaked as he moved. He was focused on a task in front of him, as his worn hands worked tirelessly. So many scars freckled his skin, showing his long tenure as Captain. He had trained many novices that excitedly joined the force, and as a result, accidents happened constantly—including some of his own. Zimyn helped bandage more of his father's wounds than he liked to admit.

"I am an old man with too much time on his hands. I needed to get creative."

Zimyn raised a brow as he tried to make sense of what he was looking at. There were small cubes of ice all over the table situated on a cold plate so they didn't melt. An assortment of tools laid out beside it. Zimyn approached the scene, removing the books and blankets from the opposite chair.

"Are you creating a model with ice?"

"Exactly that," he said enthusiastically, his hands practically shaking in excitement as he used a small knife to shape the ice. "Wood has become too easy. I needed a challenge."

Zimyn watched his father closely, appreciating the silence as he chipped away carefully. An old clock methodically ticked in the background. The quiet was so foreign for Zimyn as he had become accustomed to the loudness of his guards or the sounds of swords being clanked together in training.

"How was your visit to the West?"

Zimyn sighed, "Discouraging, especially for Ludelle. The land is in desperate need of the Undertaking, The whole court is."

"And how is little Ludelle doing?" His father asked as he brought two pieces of ice together and melded them. His eyes narrowed deeply to focus on the fine details of his model.

"She's not so little anymore."

His father waved him off. "She'll always be that little girl who stormed into the training rings before dawn to try and pick up a sword that doubled her in weight," he reminisced, as he liked to do. "One time she nicked herself and instead of crying, she tried to use her powers to seal the wound. Unfortunately, even blue blood runs warm, and it melted instantly."

Zimyn smiled to himself. That sounded like Ludelle, determined to find a solution for herself before asking for help—or never asking for help, really. He remembered that his father found her that day and brought her to a back room where he wrapped the small wound. Instead of being grateful, she had ignored Zimyn for days after, saying that his father thought her weak because of the way Zimyn treated her. To prove her wrong, Zimyn threw snowballs at her. She retaliated by throwing shards of her ice at him. They both ended up with sliced arms and legs.

"Has she chosen her betrothed?"

Zimyn whipped his head to his father, who had a knowing smirk on his face. "Why do you think I would know that?"

He whistled. "So quickly deflecting. Shouldn't the Captain of the Guard know who the Queen will choose to sleep next to each night?"

"Are you worried her husband will stab her in her sleep?"

"I am not the one worried." His father brought together more pieces, and slowly, the model was becoming clearer to Zimyn. A chair, with small crafted details mirroring the throne Ludelle sat on.

"She'll make the right choice for the Court at large. That is what's most important."

"Duty to the crown?"

"Responsibility for her people," Zimyn corrected.

His father got up, the old chair almost tipping over before Zimyn stopped it. His father had become oblivious to his surroundings as he narrowed his attention. On a window sill sat a snow globe. One Zimyn was familiar with, having seen it everyday growing up.

His father brought it over. "I gave this to your mother."

Zimyn shook it, watching the snow fall over the castle that was depicted inside. "Mother loved it. She always stared at it."

"Yes, with me staying inside the castle, and her here, we spent such little time together. It's one of my biggest regrets."

"She never held that against you," Zimyn said earnestly. "Every time you had a chance to come for dinner or for a quick break, her eyes glowed with delight."

His father gently smiled, clearly picturing her face. His mother had meant the world to the both of them. When she got sick and could barely move, each of them made sure that one of them was with her at all times to keep her company. Even when she could no longer communicate her needs, Zimyn could always tell when she wanted her husband by the way she fondly stared at the snow globe.

"She was my salvation in so many ways. She reminded me every day that I was more than just my duty to this court. That's what this snow globe was. It was a reminder that although the castle held a piece of my heart, she held it all."

Zimyn swallowed, trying to think of something to say but could barely form a word. "Why are you telling me this?" he barely choked out, his voice wavering.

His father sat back down as he got to work. The cabin walls felt constricting as Zimyn waited for him to respond. "Because your heart is much larger than your role as Captain." His father stopped and looked into Zimyn's glacial blue eyes, his father's a shade darker than his, "And because...your heart is at a crossroads."

"I've made my decision already," Zimyn said, with no room for additional argument.

Zimyn's father nodded, staring down at his model.

"Love is not simple. It requires sacrifice. Your mother sacrificed so much so I could do what I was born to do. I never took that lightly, especially when you came into the picture." His face turned solemn. "I would have sacrificed my very soul so that she could still be here today. Unfortunately, it doesn't work that way, so I spent every second that I could with her when we had it."

"Was it worth it?"

"Yes, but you knew that already."

His father had been trying to get Zimyn to stay as soon as Zimyn told him he wanted to leave. It's not that his father didn't support his decision to travel, but he assumed Zimyn was doing it for the wrong reasons—that he was running away.

Zimyn admired his parent's love, but everyone was not so privileged to experience such a simple, quiet love like they had. Zimyn and Ludelle—even if he stayed—would never be simple.

Seven

Her prayer's to the Weather Gods must have been answered, as in the days following her return from the western village, a sprinkle of snow flurries were reported and the meat was safely transferred inland, preventing fears of famine. One less thing for Ludelle to stress about, at least. Balvan had applauded the way she handled herself and her court. Ludelle didn't need his praise.

By the castle, the snow came down faster, the ground already covered in a thin coat of it. A blessing, the halls had chanted, a sign of good luck for Queen Ludelle's Undertaking! Sveta had sung her praises, too. For Ludelle, it meant nothing more than a job accomplished.

Ludelle stared up at the gray sky, snowflakes landing on her pale skin, slowly melting away. The droplets of water dripped down her face, cleansing her. The smell of pine filled her nostrils. It revitalized her. Brought back the energy she craved with only days away from the Undertaking. She would need every bit of strength to get her through it. She would need a drink to get her through the matchmaking session that Balvan had scheduled for her. He thought it would be a positive sign for the people to hear that she was carefully considering all her options, using her time to interrogate the men, one of whom would be sat at her side for the rest of her life.

For now though, she ignored that line of thought. Her future could wait for a few minutes. It was not everyday that she had time alone like this, usually someone only feet away keeping their eyes on her. She had snuck away for this small sliver of freedom.

"I've never grown tired of the peace of snow."

Ludelle jumped even though she recognized his voice immediately—except maybe that was the reason her heart missed a beat.

She didn't face Zimyn, yet. "Snow can be deadly, too."

She could hear him smirk from behind her, the crunch of twigs and leaves growing louder as he neared. "Like they say, each snowflake is unique, multifaceted...just like people."

Ludelle groaned, picking at the individual pieces of pines, sap coating her fingers. "That's horrendous."

"I was going for inspirational."

"Well you *inspired* me to decree an order that you no longer can utter a word."

"Oh, but who would be there to warn you that you have chocolate on your face before an important meeting."

She snapped her attention towards him, throwing the pine needles against his armored chest, the ice scales looking clean and newly polished. "That was one time!"

He wiped them away, but one stuck to his hair that he didn't notice. "We can't all be perfect, Ludelle."

Ludelle sauntered over to him, her dress dragging against the dirt, but she didn't care. She plucked the pine needle loose. "Apparently not."

"See? We would each be doomed without the other—"

Ludelle saw the moment he noticed his error. The way he cringed at his own words.

It pained her to consider a future with him no longer there beside her. He had been there through it all. Every lashing from her parents, every boring lesson, every sickness. As the weight of her crown crushed her, he was there to alleviate it, to take it on alongside her. She refused to trap him, though. He deserved the life he dreamed.

"We'll survive," she responded. "The world deserves to see your bright smile. It would be unfair to keep it hidden."

"You know?" he asked carefully.

"I know."

Zimyn breathed deeply, rubbing his face and shagging his hair. He stepped up so close to her, their chests touched. He lifted her chin upwards so she was staring right into those dangerous eyes. "I'm sorry."

His words died out. Once again, they found themselves in this situation where their bodies stood too close, where one more step would leave no more space between them. The way he stared at her lips, which must have turned even bluer than usual, left her frozen. His own chest was pumping hard, as if trying to take in any breath because his own body forgot how to.

"I—" he started.

"We can't—" she pleaded.

She willed her eyes to stop the tears that begged to be shed. Because even though the snow was their only witness, Ludelle could not allow them to take that final step—not now. Even if it was all that she desired and craved. Individual snowflakes might be unique, but once they were packed together they could no longer be distinguished. They weren't as special as they convinced themselves to be.

She loved him, deeply and wholeheartedly. Sometimes she thought his love ran through her veins, instead of icy powers, because that was how ingrained Zimyn was into her body and soul.

He had taken over as Captain because of his strong capability and he would stand in front of any blade to save her. But she could never say the same. She would never be able to sacrifice herself for him because of her position, and that was not fair. She had not been there for him the way he was for her. He deserved to walk freely without that weight any longer.

She had to let him go.

Tears now fell in earnest, and she didn't try to stop them or wipe them away. This one final moment of vulnerability needed to be shared. He took her in, every broken part of her.

She didn't have the words to release him, though. Not yet. She had to figure out what she wanted—no, *needed*—from him before he left her. She stormed away from him, her heart shattering into fragments of ice, sharp enough to pierce.

He slammed the door behind him. His guards stopped eating their dinners to flick their eyes to the cause of commotion. Zimyn's anger had become so strong that his vision blurred.

"Did Kotyn try to eat your hand again?" Flix joked.

He knew the words were said light-heartedly, and he knew that he shouldn't take his frustration out on his guards but he snapped.

"Shouldn't you be patrolling the back gardens?"

Flix rested his legs on the long table, as another guard quickly swiped his plate away so as to not get dirt on it. "I'm not taking the bait. You know that I don't have a night shift today. Something must be really wrong if you're getting it mixed up in your head." He took a big bite of his bread roll, talking with his mouth full. "I think we all know who it's about, too."

The other guards seated at the long table nodded.

"If I'm so obvious," he said as he stole his own bread roll from someone's plate, "why are you asking?"

Novus stepped in, pouring a small glass of clear liquid that he shoved into Zimyn's hand. "Out of respect. We want you to say it, to trust us enough with your sorrows like we trust you with ours."

Zimyn gave Flix a quick look, trying to read if the other guards knew of his upcoming departure; he shook his head.

It could wait then. Besides, he needed to be clear-headed to make such a large announcement. They all deserved that much at least.

Zimyn swished the liquor before downing it. His eyes stung again, not used to drinking since he always needed to be on alert. He took the bottle from Novus' hand and poured another. The second shot went down more smoothly, and the burn coated his throat nicely.

All eyes were on him expectantly as if any moment from now he would break down into tears as his heart bled out. No, he wouldn't do that. There would be no point, speaking about it wouldn't staunch the wound.

"I am your Captain. I share your sorrows, but you do not need to bear the weight of mine." He tried smiling, but his mouth started to feel detached from his body.

Pyro said from his spot along the back wall, "You don't have to do it alone."

But he did.

Once, long ago, he thought that he would have Ludelle by his side for the rest of their days. Not just as her Captain, but as her talisman that would serve her as decreed by the Weather Gods. His purpose was to keep her flesh safe and her heart whole because they were each other's life source, one could not breathe without the other.

That was when he accepted his future fate as Captain because it meant being by her. Now, he knew that could never be true. He needed to leave.

Eight

Waking up the next day and dressing in one of her finest gowns had been a challenge for Ludelle. Her maid pinched and prodded until her cheeks were tinged with a faded blue hue, her white hair shining with a dusting of glitter, and her dress clung perfectly to her tired body. The tight bodice straightened her back uncomfortably, but at least she looked resplendent. The silver beading that covered practically every inch of fabric weighed more than it had a right to, and the high neckline accentuated her long neck, while her exposed arms were also covered in glitter and rhinestones. The seamstress had said it was to mirror her guards' scales, to show the men vying for her hand that she had a whole force of people behind her.

A pretty sentiment.

A knock came from her door, causing Kotyn's ears to perk up. She jumped down from her stoop near the window to stand beside Ludelle as if protecting her from danger. Ludelle leaned over, even if her movements were restricted, and scratched behind the large cat's soft ears. She nudged her head so Ludelle could reach the exact spot she liked best. A spoiled beast, but Kotyn deserved it.

"Come in," Ludelle announced, as she adjusted a silver bracelet around her wrist.

Balvan trudged in with his usual piles of paper in his hands and a pen tucked behind his ear. Ludelle would have laughed if it weren't for the fact that she was being forced to entertain all the nobles because of him.

His eyes blinked a few times and scoured the room, as if just recognizing where he was after being so lost in whatever he had been reading on his way over. He took in Ludelle as she stood in front of the mirror, her bed that had dresses laying all over it, and Kotyn who was ready to pounce. "I hope that barn animal is more useful beyond giving...*cuddles*."

Kotyn hissed, stalking towards him. Ludelle gave Balvan some credit; he didn't balk even when she started sniffing him, stretching her maw towards his neck, her sharp teeth ready to clamp down on his throat to prove exactly how useful she could be. She backed away when she accepted that he wasn't a real threat, but not before swatting her tail, startling him enough to drop everything in his hands.

Ludelle chuckled. "How may I help you, Balvan?"

He was on his knees, compiling everything and muttering profanities to himself. Kotyn just yawned and went back to her nap.

"I'm here to escort you, Queen Ludelle."

Usually her Captain would be the one to do that. Ludelle wondered if Zimyn told Balvan he was unable to or if Balvan urged against having the nobles see them together.

Either way, she could escort herself. When she told Balvan as much, he waved her off.

"None of that today. Your stubbornness is not productive to the crown."

"And your inability to keep formal documents straight is helping...how?" Ludelle picked up one of the papers that had landed near her feet, seeing the royal insignia. Before she could read through it, Balvan snatched it away. "Is that not something I should be reading?"

He shook his head. "No, no. Those are just trash. Someone complaining about something, a child asking that you pray to the Weather Gods for a new toy."

Ludelle put her hands on her hips, the beads pressing into her skin. "That sounds like something I should be aware of."

"Don't trouble yourself. Your father always had me take care of this nonsense."

"I'm not my father, and I don't appreciate that you assumed that I would rule the same way." Her father—and by extension, her mother—cared more for their own comfort than the comfort of the court. Ludelle refused to be the same.

Balvan leaned against her bed. "I had asked you before. You must have been off daydreaming, so I figured you had no issue with it."

"Well don't do that in the future," she retorted sharply. "Until words have left my mouth, keep asking. Agreed?" She tilted her head to the side, waiting for him to challenge her.

They stared each other down, but she would not let Balvan win this.

"Alright, I'll make sure you receive all correspondence moving forward. We must go now."

He outstretched his hand, and Ludelle reluctantly took it

"Any standouts?" He asked, as he guided her down the hall. Her stride was much shorter in such a tight dress, but she didn't allow it to make her look weak. She kept her head high, as if her slow stride was intentional.

"You know where my head is at," she responded.

"Lord Cirrus is not the match you have concocted in your head. Don't you find him too weak-minded? You'll get bored so quickly."

"I find him to be just fine. He's charming enough to hold an audience, which is a great asset. Don't you always say I lack that easiness that the people seek? He fits that role."

"I just think there are better options in that room. His family's past is...off-putting, to say the least. Just keep your eyes and ears open to them all. His combat training is lackluster I've been told, and I know you gravitate towards brutes."

"I'll make sure that I pay close attention then during their training test, tomorrow," Ludelle gritted out. On top of this session today, Balvan had set up some time for the nobles to prove themselves as honorable fighters. He believed that her husband should be an extra layer of protection.

Satisfied with himself, Balvan led her onwards as she prepared herself to enter the lion's cage.

The gathering room had been transformed from its usual simplicity to true finery. Ice crystals hung from the ceiling, the peeking sun from the windows glistening against them, creating a mosaic of reflections against outrageous sculptures of ice. Mountains, trees, the castle, but the most ostentatious being the bust of her head. It was hideous. The craftsmanship not lacking, just...it felt wrong in this room with all these men who sought her like a prize. Had they been ogling at it as they waited for her?

Plus, it didn't seem wise to be using up so much ice to make these obscene decorations. They should be preserving it, especially as the power quickly depleted. She took note to speak with Balvan about this would-be offense.

As soon as she passed through the door, the nobles stood up and fanned around her, each bowing and trying to speak to her, desperate to make a good first impression. One of them stayed back, splayed on the back of the blue velvet couch with his legs crossed. She recognized him immediately as Lord Mitah. He looked comfortable and unperturbed by her presence. She understood his strategy immediately, and unfortunately for him, a lack of care did not amuse her or draw her in like he undoubtedly hoped. Or perhaps, he was still bitter about the card game he lost to her when they were younger.

Guards flanked each corner, but Zimyn wasn't one of them. *Good*. It was better this way. She wouldn't be distracted.

Balvan had already left her, too, saying she needed to do this on her own.

"Can I pour you a drink, Queen Ludelle?" One of the nobles asked as he made his way towards the liquor cabinet.

Each of them had a large glass of their own. "Well since you seem to take no issue with being heavy-handed with the castle's collection, I suppose the Queen should join in, shouldn't she?" Some of them winced, clearly ashamed. Others cheered her unabashedly.

Taking a swig, she downed the whole thing in one go, then pointed for another. The noble happily obliged, doubling the amount.

"I appreciate a woman who is unafraid to enjoy the festivities. My mother had always declined even a sip of a drink because she worried too much about appearing unsightly. She thought a woman with alcohol in her breath was a disgrace."

Ludelle narrowed her eyes at the backhanded insult. "What's your name?"

"Lord Finch."

"Lord Finch." she smiled, clinking her glass against his while he smiled back cheerily. She leaned forward and whispered into his ears. "Insult me again, and I will stab you with the bones of your dead mother." She then straightened herself, the other nobles now watching closely. "Guards, please escort Lord Finch out of the castle."

Lord Finch's eyes widened as two guards hauled him away. She could have sworn a tear dripped down his face, and she loved the sight of it.

So...she had only three nobles left to pick from, now. Those three now had put their drinks down on the crystal table that was situated between the two couches. One had his hands behind his back as if he worried that she would chop them off at any moment. It was a pleasing feeling to be respected.

"Please sit." They all stood around unsure, scratching their heads, so she said more forcefully. "Pick a seat and sit down."

They listened this time, practically tripping over themselves to find a spot. Amusing would put it lightly. She liked the power she had in these situations. How easy it was to get people to do as she told them to. One of the guards in the corner coughed, as if trying to cover a laugh because he noticed it, too.

Ludelle kept standing though, not letting herself be in a vulnerable position. There were too many instances where men would think they were at the same level as her when she sat down. Plus, her dress made it difficult, but they didn't need to know that.

"You are all here to court me, so do your best," she said plainly, shrugging nonchalantly as if she didn't want to be here. A stain on her day.

Lord Mitah quickly took his chance. He was the first out of his seat, and gracefully stepped up to her. His gray suit with silver thread complemented her dress. A lucky happenstance.

"Queen Ludelle," he bowed. "May we sit in the corner and chat?"

Ludelle obliged him since she had no other choice in the matter, as they took a spot next to the desserts table. There was everything that a person could dream of: tarts with the freshest fruit, biscuits covered in silver and white icing, and her favorite chocolate cake, which she had to resist.

The other nobles deflated back on the couch, beating themselves up for not getting to her first. Developing patience was an important aspect of the future consort, so she felt no guilt.

"You are a beauty just like they say," the noble said, as he assessed her, taking stock of all the assets she left on display. The slit that left her leg exposed, and his eyes trailed upwards until they landed on her face.

"Flattery won't get you far." she told him, as she straightened her dress. Sitting in it was practically impossible but she adjusted herself to make it work.

"Then, we shall skip all the pleasantries and move on to more serious topics."

"What topics did you have in mind?" She asked, her pulse quickening.

"The issue of your Undertaking, of course."

"My Undertaking is my burden. There is no reason to harp on it further than I already do."

He stretched over and picked a gooseberry and vanilla custard tart. Did he know that was Zimyn's favorite?

"Well...it concerns me, too, if I am chosen as your betrothed, as I will be the one on the other side thrown into potential danger." He took a bite, the custard sticking to his lips until he dragged his tongue across it. He moaned lightly. "Has your Captain prepared you?"

"The court's Captain has been training me since childhood. I am more than ready." She didn't appreciate him questioning her abilities—and Zimyn's—all in one breath.

Although, Ludelle never considered the other side of this. That perhaps the nobles did not want to be in the position of putting their life on the line for a test that rested on Ludelle's shoulders. She assumed anyone offered the opportunity would just gladly take it.

"What if the danger is of the mind?" Seeing the confusion on her face, he continued, impressed with himself that he'd caught her off guard. "What if instead of a physical threat, your Undertaking strips you bare? Your heart and soul ripped, while you have to piece it back together. Are you ready for that?"

Ludelle shook her head frantically. "There has never been such an Undertaking. I assure you my fighting skills will be tested in some way or another." Though she wished it wouldn't. "And even if it is of the mind, I think I have proven myself to you already. I'm sure you remember the tantrum that you threw after I beat you in such a simple game all those years ago."

His jaw tensed as he brushed the crumbs from his suit. "I hope you are correct, because I wouldn't take a chance on you otherwise."

Ludelle gasped, prepared to give him a lashing of her own. How dare he question his Queen? But she didn't have a chance before the doors opened and Zimyn walked in.

Nine

Zimyn didn't want to be here. In fact, he purposefully assigned Flix to take his place because he couldn't stomach watching these men peacock themselves in order to win her hand. Ludelle was not a prize, but a gift that one laid their soul to.

Which is why he had spent the last hour pacing and feeling guilty for leaving her to those vultures. She didn't need him protecting her, but she did need someone supporting her. Someone with her best interest in mind.

Ludelle's attention had snapped his way when the door clicked shut behind him, but the Queen quickly recovered and turned away. Lord Mitah barely spared him a glance before he rested his hand on her exposed thigh, like he was staking his claim. Her white flesh against his tawny skin made Zimyn's heart clench. Ludelle tried swatting Lord Mitah's hand away, but the noble wouldn't budge.

Zimyn relieved Flix of his position in one of the corners and surveyed the other nobles who seemed to have abandoned their drinks. *Strange.* Zimyn had been told that four nobles would be present.

One either didn't make it, or he was a fool who got on Ludelle's bad side. Zimyn wagered it was the latter.

With the harp player softly trailing her fingers through the strings, he couldn't hear the conversation as the noble whispered in Ludelle's ear, but from Ludelle's fisted hands, he could tell she was displeased. Would it be foolish of him to try and rescue her? Most definitely—but it didn't stop him from fantasizing about it. How easy it would be to yank on the noble's suit collar and slice his sword across his fragile skin, until only shreds remained.

Lord Cirrus sighed. "Do you think it would be rude to interrupt?"

The other one, Lord Aeden, his gray hair a ruffled mess, shrugged. "She's Queen, I think it's wise we wait."

Zimyn found himself nodding and immediately stopping when Novus smirked at him from across the room. Zimyn gave his guard a stern look in return.

"Waiting doesn't seem like the prime strategy. If I want to call her mine, then I need to step in. Consequences be damned. "

"Insulting her isn't either." The noble that seemed to not give a shit about this at all responded. He began unbuttoning his shirt as if the room was hot. Zimyn had to restrain himself from slapping him for being so uncaring. He was in the presence of their Queen and thought it okay to conduct himself like a bored child.

Lord Cirrus groaned, messing with his diamond cufflinks; ones he likely took with zero cost because of his family.

Although diamonds were special and created abundant trade, they were not as rare as the sapphire—the court's sanctioned gem directly from the Weather Gods. There were so few of them within the court, and all of them were within the castle walls.

Zimyn's sword had a sapphire decorating its hilt, though the sword was more for show than for actual combat. It had been passed down from his father and all Captains before him. It was blessed by the minister each year after the Undertaking. Zimyn usually kept it hidden in his room. It was too ostentatious, in his opinion. He also had no loyalty to the Gods. He always felt that the gemstones were just another way to control the people, a physical sign of the Weather Gods good intentions that others believed. Yet, at the end of the day, the Weather Gods still preferred humbling them each year by threatening them with their extinction. He never voiced those opinions, knowing that Ludelle needed to have full faith in the Gods in order to keep fighting for their court. He respected that about her.

Lord Cirrus slid down on his couch, his shoes dragging the fur rug and making a mess. "I think they have had enough time."

Zimyn practically drilled a hole in the back of the noble's head with the way he stared him down as the noble made his way to Ludelle. The three of them exchanged a few words before the two nobles switched spots. The remaining noble on the couch downed his drink.

Zimyn took a deep breath, preparing to endure a long few hours.

Ludelle couldn't take it. She could barely focus on what any of these nobles were saying, and that was a problem since she only had a few days left before having to make a decision. Why was Zimyn even here?

"—and I just think I could level up the decor of this castle. It could use my keen eye."

Ludelle shook her head at Lord Cirrus. "What?"

"I was saying," he enunciated slowly as if she was daft. The music in the background had crescendoed, growing in intensity. It was her favorite harpist, the one who had played at the ball, too. One she discovered on a visit to the Lightning Court years ago. Although the court had innovated, there was something about the grandness yet simplicity of the harp that called to Ludelle. "That the castle needs to be updated. I feel like I'm in a hollow cove, not the home of royalty."

Ludelle peered around the room. All the decorations for this gathering had given it some character for sure, though she supposed the actual foundation of it all looked plain. "Are you insulting my ancestors' design choices?"

"Yes," he said simply, rubbing his fingers against the fabric of the chaise, his face turning in disgust, unimpressed with the quality, Ludelle guessed.

Ludelle didn't even hate the fact that he honed in on such a mundane thing. It was better than trying to sway any of her political choices. That's why he would be the perfect choice. He would allow her to rule, while he planned the parties.

"I'll take that into consideration," she said finally, resigned to let him speak.

"That includes the bedroom."

Of course it did. "What about the bedroom?"

"Well, I haven't seen it obviously, but I am very particular with how I like to sleep." He gestured to himself when Ludelle didn't respond. "Nude. I need bedding that is gentle on my fragile skin." Skin he had dotted with small diamonds along his neck and hands, which matched her own glittering arms. She wondered who told him that she would be dressed like this.

Ludelle didn't even know what to say at this point. This man had disillusioned himself into thinking he would even be allowed to sleep in the same bed as her. The castle had many bedrooms. Her future husband could find his own.

"I think I should move on to the final noble," Ludelle suggested, but Lord Cirrus only scooted closer, his thigh now pressed against hers.

"You can't get rid of me that easily."

"Now you just are insulting my power."

"No, I'm complimenting my determination. Two different things." He reached over her, his body extending towards the dessert table as he plucked up a piece of chocolate covered fruit. His body smelled of woodsy musk, like he ran through the outdoors and absorbed it into his light skin.

He took a bite of his treat, and juice oozed down his mouth. He slowly licked his lips, savoring the taste of it.

"I'd prefer if you didn't eat that way in front of me." Ludelle's stomach churned at his failed attempt at being sensual.

"Are you not used to a man who is confident with his tongue?"

"Confidence does not equal competence," Ludelle shrugged casually.

He chuckled. "I like you."

That shot a pang through her. She didn't know what to make of that. She wasn't trying to have the nobles like her, just tolerate her—because feelings would be messy. But she had a role, and she needed Zimyn to know she had this under control, so there would be no doubt in his mind when he left.

She leaned down and whispered in his ear as she dragged her sharp nails down his neck, the diamonds popping off as she did. To anyone watching, the gesture would appear genial. "I would hate to disappoint."

Ten

The encounter between Lord Cirrus and Ludelle put Zimyn on edge. He prepared for the noble to escalate the situation as Ludelle clearly taunted him, as she normally did. He would happily escort Lord Cirrus out of the castle, grab his glittering arms and pull him away from her forever. Even the harpist had stopped playing, anticipating the worst. But Ludelle's expressions changed from determined, to confused, to sultry. It was the bit in the middle that Zimyn held onto—the subtle change in demeanor that most would have missed, but he wasn't most people.

Lord Cirrus bowed gracefully, like only a noble was taught to do, and said, "I'll see you at our combat skills test, Queen Ludelle." He quirked his lips, as he bent down to kiss the back of her hand. His lips lingered for too long. "Save me a moment alone? My throwing could use some help."

Ludelle nodded stiffly but didn't give him the pleasure of uttering a single word.

All eyes were on the last noble who still slouched on the couch. When Lord Aeden noticed that everyone was waiting, he jumped up and headed to the Queen.

Ludelle's white eyes glossed over as they sat together, the circles under her eyes visible. She was growing tired. Zimyn wanted to pull her away from this room like he did when they were children. When Ludelle had been stuffed into dresses that made it hard to breathe, Zimyn would join his father to the same events as his shadow as a way for Zimyn to learn. When the adults got into tense arguments about topics that went flying over his head, Zimyn would reach out his hand to his friend and lead her away. She never hesitated. They would find themselves in the kitchens for a snack or in the game room to play a round of cards. Either way, they found comfort in each other's company. They both knew they would face consequences when their parents discovered what they did, but for that short time, they could be children together, a symphony of laughing and teasing that filled the quiet halls.

Zimyn had to hold back his smile at the memories.

As Lord Aeden and Ludelle parted ways, Ludelle took a deep breath and stood. Novus immediately went to open the door for her. She gave the nobles a quick thank you and told them she was excited to see them present their fighting skills in the training ring, though her tone did not exude that same excitement.

Only Zimyn, the harpist, and the nobles remained in the room. He patiently waited until the harpist left with her sheets of music before he clicked the door shut and locked it.

"Going to scare us away?" Lord Cirrus said. His eyes were trained on the now empty glass of the drink he had just gulped down.

"Something like that," Zimyn grumbled.

"Should we even be listening to you?" The first noble asked, the one who eagerly took the opportunity to touch Ludelle without permission. "We outrank you in status. Quite frankly, you should be taking *our* orders."

Zimyn now recognized him as Lord Mitah, the worst of the bunch. His quick dismissal of Zimyn only proved how little he cared for those below his station.

"You'll listen!" Zimyn fumed, his skin flushing in anger. "One of you may become her husband, but I will always be her Captain. Her trust begins and ends with me." They didn't know the truth yet. No one but a few did. His departure was a secret. He breathed in deeply, lowering his voice as he bit out, "One wrong move from any of you, and I will hand over every blade I own to Ludelle and watch as she slices your body into pieces."

Lord Mitah wiggled his fingers in a mocking manner. "Scary."

"You think I'm joking?"

"I think this is exhausting." The others nodded. "As future King—"

"Consort," Zimyn corrected.

"I will simply banish you from the castle." He said haughtily. "Then there's nothing you'll be able to do."

Good thing Zimyn would be long gone, but even if he weren't leaving. "Ludelle wouldn't allow it."

"Are you sure?" Lord Cirrus said, as he picked off the loose diamonds from his skin and threw them on the rug. "The people need confidence that the Queen and her consort are a solid unit. If you are around, everyone will keep questioning what you mean to each other, just like they do now. Queen Ludelle will never be taken seriously for her actual actions but instead for the rumors that trail her like a ghost."

Zimyn blinked back the shock at Lord Cirrus' words. The Lord almost seemed concerned for Ludelle, like he actually cared for her wellbeing.

Zimyn had always known how detrimental their relationship could be to her image as Queen. He hoped the people trusted her motives enough, that she would only act in the best interest of her Court. That was how he knew she operated at least, but not everyone had such an intimate understanding of her like he did. It was why his leaving benefitted them both.

"Queen Ludelle is more than capable of convincing the people of her hard work. The fact that you mistrust her reveals exactly how little you think of her." Zimyn said as he stepped closer, his heavy boots thumping on the icy floor. He knew he shouldn't speak like this to Lord Cirrus, he knew that Ludelle would get angry at him for it, but he couldn't help it. "Shoving your status at me does not exempt you from being thrown in a prison cell for such blasphemy."

"You threaten me?"

"Do you feel threatened?" Zimyn shot back. Lord Cirrus was now only a hair's breadth away, but the noble relented, taking a step back.

He knew that he was in the front running of becoming consort, and he wouldn't let Zimyn jeopardize it. *Smart.*

Lord Mitah, on the other hand, stepped forward and shoved Zimyn to the ground, the ice slamming in Zimyn's lower back. He foolishly wasn't expecting anyone to actually get physical, thinking the occasion to be too proper, but Zimyn now reached for his sword, only for the noble to beat him to it as he swiped it from his sheath. The noble held the long blade against his throat. Any small movement would cause him to slice himself.

The noble laughed in his face. "You're useless. You can't even protect yourself, so how can you protect her?"

The remaining nobles managed to pull the blade out of his grip but Lord Mitah, still on top of him, spat in his face. Zimyn flinched, but he didn't even bother putting up a fight. Everything he said was true.

"Animals!" Balvan reprimanded, a red flush of anger blooming against his cheeks. "Should I bring Kotyn in here, too?"

The noble and Zimyn quickly scrambled to their feet, like two children being caught by their parents.

Balvan continued, "I had more faith in you Lord Mitah, but maybe I was wrong."

Zimyn cleared his throat. "It was my fault, Balvan."

"You," Balvan pointed. "Keep quiet."

Zimyn pressed his lips tight.

"All of you to your rooms. There will be enough time for this during training tomorrow. I expect you all can manage without causing a raucous?" The wide eyed nobles all nodded. "Zimyn, you can stay."

Zimyn's shoulders dropped as the nobles snickered. When it was finally just the two of them, Balvan stretched himself across the couch, his arms anchored behind his head, not a worry in sight, acting as if he owned the room. Zimyn stayed where he was.

Balvan sighed. "You and I are on the same side, you know. We both want to see Ludelle succeed. We both know that the Undertaking is the key to that success."

Zimyn ground his teeth. He would not say anything to Balvan, because as much as he agreed with him, he wouldn't admit it out loud. They may have the same motives—to see Ludelle prosper—but Zimyn approached it entirely differently.

"You're the one who chose to give it all up. The title, the friends, the home...Her." Balvan swiped a pastry and bit into it. "I applaud you for it, actually. It's one of the noblest things you've done. Braver than I ever was." Zimyn didn't understand what he meant by that. "Don't mess it up for her by getting in the way. Can you do that for her?"

The question was so simple, but his response would alter everything. Because of course he would do anything required to see Ludelle happy. Another part of him wanted to never leave her side because she was his happiness. Without her, his life would be so much emptier. These future travels, although something he had desired to do for years, felt like they were filling a void because he couldn't have her.

"I don't answer to you." Zimyn said at last.

Balvan raised his brows. "Well, I can answer that question, easily. I'll do anything necessary to have Ludelle win her Undertaking and pick a strong consort."

Eleven

Ludelle, Balvan, and Zimyn were all on the sidelines as the nobles warmed up. Ludelle got to the rings early to be able to do some practice throws in private. She hit the targets perfectly. Three times in a row. She hoped that her luck would stick now that she had an audience.

"Do these nobles even train?" Zimyn asked. His arms were crossed in front of him, already on the defensive.

"Of course they do," Balvan replied. "What else is a noble to do with their time?"

Ludelle snorted. They both whipped their heads in her direction.

"What?" she bit out. "It's true. These nobles have too much time on their hands. I want to be impressed."

"How much do you want to bet that it'll take less than ten minutes before one of them is hurt?" Zimyn's eyes practically sparkled with the anticipation of it.

They did this often, especially when they were younger. Whenever they had to attend a boring meeting, they bet on something. No coin was involved, just bragging rights. At first, they kept things reasonable. A noble would lose their temper or Balvan would drop his pen. That became too easy, so they started betting on the most outlandish scenarios. If her father would chip a tooth, or if a bird would somehow fly through the room. One time, they bet that Kotyn would hop on the table. She did once. That was the last time she was allowed to attend any official court meetings. Ludelle thought Kotyn became happier after that decision.

It felt nice to be back to that friendly companionship; a relief to have dispersed that tension. Sure, she was still upset that he didn't tell her the truth but deep down she understood why. More importantly, their time was limited, and she didn't want to spend that time in a fight. He was her person. She wanted to savor every second she had left.

"You're on!" Ludelle said. "And I'll even bet on it being Mitah."

Zimyn reached out his hand, and they shook on it. She let her grasp linger a moment longer than she should have, taking in his warmth.

"Are you two done?" Balvan reprimanded, and she pulled away from Zimyn. "I think it's time to begin."

Zimyn began some drills with the nobles. Ludelle stayed back to observe.

"I wouldn't underestimate Lord Mitah as much as you have been. He's a strong match for you," Balvan said so only she could hear.

"Lord Mitah has an icicle up his ass because his ego is too weak."

Balvan sighed, "You need to take time and reflect on who exactly you want by your side. Someone who compliments your abilities."

"You already know Lord Cirrus is my option. *You're* the one who is making it difficult by not accepting that and refusing to explain why."

"He offers you nothing," he said too sharply to mean nothing. Ludelle was beginning to think there was a history there that Balvan was keeping to himself. She didn't care to push him on it though.

"His family runs the diamond mines. He'd be a strong asset to have in the castle," Ludelle contested. "Lord Mitah on the other hand is just a spoiled noble who cares about nothing but himself and a pretty title."

"Then I guess when it's time to go to the divine temple room, you can submit your choice to the Weather Gods. I just hope you don't regret it."

The training session had been a disaster. Lord Mitah had, in fact, gotten himself hurt via a gash across his palm, all because he thought it was a good idea to toss a sword in the air, then try to catch it.

"He didn't throw it high enough and he grabbed the blade as it fell down," Ludelle recounted to Helena and Villeta.

They were sitting in the small dining area attached to her rooms. She usually used this space whenever she could eat on her own, but she invited the two of them to join her.

Helena and Villeta, whether intentionally or not, complemented each other's outfits. Helena's light hair down while wearing a black gown, while Villeta's dark waves draped over her ivory dress.

"Some men always feel the need to prove themselves," Villeta said as she cut through her steak. Red blood oozed out of it.

"That's why women are better," Helena beamed. Villeta gave her cousin a peck on her cheek, then fed her the piece of steak.

Ludelle's heart ached at the ease between them. She craved that, but she accepted that it would no longer be in her future, which brought her to the reason they were here.

"I need some advice."

That piqued their interest.

Ludelle's face heated, already uncomfortable with the vulnerability she was about to emit. "I..." She shook her head and started again, pretending to be in a meeting with Balvan. She donned a Queenly stature. "As you know, myself and Zimyn have a connection. One that had always been beyond friendship."

Helena snorted. Ludelle gave her a sharp glare.

"What?" Helena said. "That's obvious to anyone with eyes."

"Well," Ludelle continued as she picked at her plate. "He's leaving right after my Undertaking to travel the courts."

Their faces both saddened.

"I'm sorry," Villeta said with comfort. She reached out and squeezed Ludelle's hand. "That must hurt."

Ludelle cleared her throat, not allowing the emotion to consume her.

"It does, but I want Zimyn to be happy more than anything, so I support his decision. We have never been together intimately. We agreed to wait until after my marriage so that there would be no guilt in the action and it would make it easier for me to pick someone besides him."

"Oh." Helena squeaked. "I always thought you both were secretly ravishing each other."

Ludelle smiled. "That was the plan once I was married, but now...I don't feel a reason to wait. Should we just go for it?"

Both of their mouths gaped open, and Ludelle immediately regretted the questions. Of course they would think that she was ridiculous. It was a stupid notion.

"Yes, go for it!" Helena yelled, like it was the most obvious thing. "You'll regret it otherwise."

Villeta nodded eagerly. "The memory of being in his arms in that intimate way will be a lasting one, especially when you love him as much as you do."

"How do you know I love him?"

"Because you are willing to sacrifice that love so he can be happy."

Ludelle sniffled and wiped away a tear that strayed down her cheek. Helena stood up and rubbed Ludelle's back.

"We'll be here once he's gone. Every step of the way."

Ludelle had never been more grateful to have her ladies in waiting. Perhaps Balvan had been right that she just needed to spend more time with them. She promised herself that she would make a better effort once her Undertaking was done. She needed these women,

Ludelle realized. They could offer a camaraderie greater than that of any consort.

Twelve

Zimyn dreamed. Even when he tried to escape Ludelle, she found a way in, like a winter chill that refused to let spring melt in. Tonight, he dreamed of simpler times, when their legs were still too short, when their royal manners were not yet fully drilled into them.

Their parents were entertaining some guests for the afternoon, leaving them both to do what they pleased—like breaking royal rules.

Zimyn was chasing Ludelle down the hall, both of them sliding against the icy floors without caution. They had just gotten back in from sledding outside where the snow was thick and tall, a storm having just raged through the court. Now, it was the calm after; at least it was supposed to be, but they always found trouble

Ludelle had stolen a dagger from the guards collection in the training room, and she was now swinging it around unsheathed. Zimyn had to duck too many times to count to avoid being sliced. He could even feel his knees bruising after he'd slipped as they'd been careless in running up the stairs.

"Ludelle you're gonna cut yourself," Zimyn cautioned her, but she was ignoring him completely as she waved her arms around, the poor nearby curtain a casualty. Ludelle's eyes widened but she didn't focus on the damage too long before she rushed off again, her long dress billowing behind her.

Zimyn desperately needed a moment to catch his breath, but he also needed to keep up with her. Even at this young age, he felt the pressure of responsibility for the princess' safety.

He tiptoed quietly and turned the corner, ready to sneak up on her, when he practically crashed right into Ludelle's grandmother, the former Queen. She looked down at him, her wrinkled skin tightening as she smiled down at him.

"You're hurt," she said plainly. When he didn't say anything back, she pointed to his neck. Zimyn swiped his hand over his throat, and sure enough, red stained his palm. He remembered the time when he first saw Ludelle's blue blood, how different she was from him and the rest of the court—a line drawn between royalty and those beneath them. For some reason though, at that moment, he didn't care that she had hurt him.

"My granddaughter is a feisty one, which means she throws caution to the wind."

Zimyn still could not speak. He had never interacted with the former Queen before. Sure, he had seen her at balls and dinners, but nothing like this.

"Ludelle is currently locked up in the washing room getting a bath for today's ball. Let's get you patched up in the meantime."

Her quarters were simpler than he expected. He had sneaked into Ludelle's parent's room once, and stepping into that had been like walking inside a sapphire gem. The walls were extravagant and gaudy. It had been suffocating.

This was a breath of fresh air. The windows open, bringing a nice breeze to the room. It was much better than the stuffy guard's quarters.

"Sit, sit," she patted the spot next to her, the lavish covers on her bed were soft on his skin. Zimyn had no idea where she got the supplies but he did as he was told. Using a damp cloth, she pressed it to his skin, and he hissed as it stung, his eyes quickly watering.

"My granddaughter is lucky to have you." Zimyn whipped his head to her, but she adjusted it back so she could keep working. "Having someone in your life, especially as royalty, that you can deeply trust is a privilege not many have." Zimyn had a suspicion she was speaking from experience, and questions were on the tip of his tongue, but she continued without elaborating. "Some find it in partners, some in their friends, some in their Captain of the Guard, and some even in their advisors." She had admitted the last part sheepishly.

"It's a Captain's job to ensure that the royal line is safe at all costs," he stated matter of factly. Even then, Zimyn understood his future role well.

With his neck craned to the side, he couldn't see the former Queen's face, but he felt her breathy laugh. "You are a smart one. Yes, that is a Captain's duty, and it is important that it is taken seriously.

But you..." she paused and stopped her work. She narrowed her eyes, really taking the time to look at him. "You and her are like looking in the mirror. Opposites of the same image. You're dedicated. She's strong-willed. You compliment each other beautifully. A perfect pair that would be unstoppable."

"Captains don't marry royalty."

The former Queen sighed as she wrapped some gauze on his now clean cut. "Yes, they do say that. But maybe...love can overcome even those old traditions that serve no one. I wished they did long ago."

Zimyn had no clue what the woman was saying. Perhaps with her old age, her mind had already started declining. How could she be in support of the two of them? It didn't make sense.

"Remember, mirrors are no longer useful after they have shattered." She cupped his cheek, her eyes turning serious. "Don't let anyone break that formidable force you two share, even when the pressure becomes too much."

Zimyn gasped awake, his back sweating and the memory from so long ago blurred away as he panted, trying to catch his breath. That had been the first time someone from the royal family had outwardly acknowledged his trajectory towards becoming Ludelle's Captain of the Guard. Even Ludelle had never said it out loud at that time, whether in denial or because she didn't care. Or maybe, like him, she didn't want to draw a line between two friends. One of royalty, the other nothing more grand than an employee.

Whatever Ludelle's reason, Zimyn was always conscious of how they came from two different worlds. How he would be up before the sun with his father, and she would roll out of bed just in time for breakfast. Yet, even then, they blended together as one force.

There was an underlying guilt to Zimyn's insistence for leaving. It was a storm that he constantly battled within; because even though Ludelle's grandmother was long gone, he still felt like he owed it to her to stay—to be the person in the court that Ludelle could trust.

Zimyn stormed into his father's cabin, not even giving him the decency to knock before he entered. He didn't know why he came here, why this was the first place he thought of going after restlessly laying in bed for too long.

All he knew was that he needed some answers. His father seemed like the right man for the job.

He noted the figurine his father had been working on, a replica of the throne. At the sight of it, Zimyn threw it against the wall and watched as it broke apart.

"Did that make you feel better?" His father said from behind him.

Zimyn heaved a breath. "No."

He itched to cause real damage. Perhaps he should have woken up one of his guards for a fight instead of coming here.

"You could use a drink, I'm sure. Unfortunately, I only have tea."

He finally faced his father who limped towards the hearth. All those years in service had done his body harm, and Zimyn hated that.

"There's no need to trouble yourself," Zimyn waved him off. "I should be going back anyways."

His father wasn't having it. "You came here for a reason. So spit it out, son."

"I—" He collected himself. He didn't even know how to approach this discussion. "Ludelle's grandmother was so much different from her parents."

"Indeed. She was a compassionate leader. I have no idea how her own son became so cruel."

"She was betrayed, though." He didn't say it as a question, and his father's lack of response proved that he was right.

"Yes, her husband tried to ruin her. I was still young then, but I was told that he tried to make a secret deal with a powerful Lord—I never learned exactly who—while trying to make her fail her Undertaking. Her husband wanted to appear as the competent ruler while she was kept in the dark. Stupid man would have doomed us all."

"But he didn't," Zimyn said cautiously.

"She stepped down right after she survived that year's Undertaking. Ludelle's father was crowned King immediately after. She had so much more to give to this court, but her time had to be cut short because of her husband's selfishness."

Looking back on that dream, Zimyn now understood it clearly. "She was scared that the same would happen to Ludelle."

"I fear it might, once she marries one of those nobles."

Zimyn shook his head, refusing to even consider that future for her. "She's strong."

"That she is."

Ludelle prepared her entire life to guarantee that she would not be so easily smited by her power-hungry betrothed. She was cunning enough to choose a consort who cared more for the comfortable lifestyle in the castle, than one who had any thoughts about the runnings of the court. That's why he knew Lord Cirrus would be the perfect match. Ludelle could control a man whose focus was more on the way *he* looked than on her.

Zimyn wiped his face, tiredness overtaking him all of a sudden. He needed to rest, the next few days would be stressful.

"I'm sorry for breaking your carving."

His father gave him a comforting pat on his shoulder. "Goodnight, Zimyn."

As he was leaving the cottage, he slammed headlong into someone, and gasped when he recognized the Queen. Zimyn steadied Ludelle before she could fall backwards, gripping her wrist while snapping out: "What are you doing here?"

She looked stunned, her white face glowing in the moonlight. "I don't know. I was going to come find you to make sure you were okay after I heard about the fight with Lord Mitah, and then I saw you leaving the castle, so I followed."

He released her and stormed past, mumbling under his breath about how foolish and dangerous it was for her to be out here at night.

She scoffed. "This is dangerous? How about the one who started a brawl with a noble with so much power that he could pay to have you thrown in the dungeons?"

"He started it." Zimyn gritted through his teeth.

"Why are you so angry?" She asked, following swiftly behind him. "You knew this day would come. *You* are the one leaving, escaping this place!"

He deflated because she was right. He knew it for so long, and it wasn't fair that he was now taking it out on her.

"I'm sorry," he apologized. "I'm just scared." For so many reasons, he was scared. Would her husband betray her? Would she forget him once she had another man by her side? Would he forget the way she made him feel just by being in her shadow?

Leaves crunched behind him as she rested her hand on his shoulder. "Don't worry about me."

"I'll always worry."

She chuckled, "I know. I also know that I'll always be safe because you taught me how to protect myself."

"Good." He brushed a stray hair behind her ear. "I'm glad I can at least provide that comfort."

Then, she did something that she hadn't done since they were little. She wrapped her arms around him. He did the same. They stood there in each other's embrace, letting the darkness cloak them.

Thirteen

Zimyn sat on his bed, a full glass of liquor in his hand. His body wanted that sip of relief, that drowning sensation to kick in. His mind had other ideas. It refused to let him bring his glass to his dry mouth because it would be admitting that he had second thoughts about everything. It proved that he didn't want to leave Ludelle alone with these vultures. Mostly, he didn't want to seem like a sop whose whole world revolved around her—that he couldn't keep himself composed, just because his heart was broken.

But, it was. He was completely torn.

He reveled in those last moments they had alone together outside his father's cabin. When the moment came to an end and they let go, it was like pulling the scales from his flesh. A dawning realization that he would never have her wholly and completely like he dreamed.

Thankfully, none of his guards disturbed him. Some rested before their night shift, while most of them were on duty. Ludelle was entertaining the nobles again, one last time before she made her final decision.

He should be walking Flix through all his new responsibilities as Captain or packing his things, but he didn't have the energy to do it.

A knock at his door shook him out of his daze. "I'm busy," he yelled. Though that might not be wise. The castle might be under attack. Or worse, Ludelle might have a sword at her throat. At the thought, he rushed to the door and meant to pull when someone was already pushing in.

Ludelle stumbled in, light glowing behind her like a goddess of death ready to take him away.

"If this is what you call busy, then I want to know what you look like when you're actually working," Ludelle teased, her voice tinged with excitement.

"I'm in no mood, Ludelle," he said. "Shouldn't you be off picking your betrothed?"

"Right, of course." She nodded as she undid the button at the front of her dress. "That's important," she replied, breathily.

His eyes widened. "What are you doing—"

She shushed him. "Quiet. I don't want the guards to hear."

Zimyn shook his head. "Hear what?" This couldn't be happening. He pinched himself. He must have had too much to drink and had fallen asleep.

Ludelle huffed in frustration when she slid the gown down her body and it got caught at her feet. She kicked it away, leaving her only in a silver slip. The straps could barely be considered pieces of thread, and the hem reached just below her knees, exposing her muscled calves—ones he helped hone. He didn't understand why the sight of them affected him so much. He's seen her legs before, but the knowledge that once she pulled off that last piece of thin fabric, it would leave her completely bare, had his mouth watering and body going tight.

Tears sprang to her eyes. "This might be all that we have." Her honesty, her sorrow at coming to a similar truth as him, completely destroyed him. He hated seeing her like this. Why must the Gods have punished them to such a fate?

"What do you want, Ludelle?" He rasped, walking backwards until he hit the edge of the bed. Even though he was Captain, his room was still small, a way to create a sense of equality among the guards.

She followed him. "You. Always you."

"That's not fair," he whispered angrily. "We promised each other we wouldn't take that step until after your Undertaking." He needed to push her away before it went too far.

"Zimyn, you'll be gone by then. This might be all we have, and I want you so desperately."

"I know," he said, exasperated because it was true, and he hated that fact. He sat on his bed, his head cradled in his hands. Because this must be a dream, a nightmare. The consequences of this would ruin her. He heard her light footsteps inching closer. She must have taken off her shoes at some point, and that made this more real.

"Look at me." She placed a long cobalt claw under his chin and lifted it up. He would forever regret doing that because the vulnerability in her white eyes—her silver pupils dilated—would forever be stamped into his mind's eye. His last bit of strength collapsed as soon as she grabbed the crown on her head and threw it on the mattress. It bounced and toppled to the floor. "I'm all yours tonight."

Zimyn breathed deeply from his nose, but his restraint was gone. He grabbed her waist and tossed her on the bed, anchoring his arms on both sides of her body. She traced the side of his face, then his lips. He took her hand and kissed the tip of her finger and then the pulsepoint of her wrist, where he could have sworn he felt her heart jump.

"Are you sure?" Because she must know the harm this would cause if someone were to find out.

"More than anything," she responded with such definitiveness. How could he say no?

Zimyn didn't hesitate as he closed the last bit of distance and pressed his lips against hers. The world around them froze. She dragged her hands along the scales on his arms. He shuddered as he felt them melt at her heat—evidence that only with her would he let his armor go.

He bit her bottom lip, and she gasped. He took the opportunity to drive his tongue into her mouth. Her tongue met his, and she was so soft, so pliant, so ready for him. She reacted perfectly to his touch, in a way no one else could. They fit together like a blade in its sheath, like they were made for each other.

"Zimyn," she moaned, as he dragged his mouth to her neck, nipping lightly at her skin, small marks of faded blue slowly appearing. "I want you lower," she demanded.

"Not yet."

If this was it, then he would take his time, learn every inch of her, so at night as he touched himself, he would be able to trace the map of her body he'd drawn in his mind.

Ludelle whined as he bit the strap of the slip and pulled it down. Growing impatient, Ludelle tried sliding it off herself, but he stopped her and held her hands above her head.

"I'm the one in control now."

"Oh, you've definitely dreamed of the day when you could say that," she crooned.

"Every night," he admitted honestly. It was the only time he would allow himself to consider it. His days were too full of reminders of his responsibility as Captain to even have time to immerse himself in the fantasies of having her in his bed.

Zimyn groaned once he finally got the dress down and her peaked nipples were freed from the garment. He could spend days lavishing them. Ludelle arched her back as he started sucking on the right, swirling the nub with his tongue. Goosebumps peppered her pale skin as she shivered.

"I *need* you lower," she begged this time, her hands desperately trying to get out his grasp, but failing.

He ignored her, focusing his attention now on her left nipple. Finally, when he had his fill of her breasts, Zimyn moved his mouth lower on her writhing body, pulling the dress down with it.

"I never knew a Queen could be so needy."

"I never knew my Captain of the Guard was so bad at listening to orders. Maybe it's time I found a new one."

Ludelle meant it as a joke, clearly, but the reality of that statement shook him enough that he needed a second to orient himself back to what was happening.

Though, once he spied her exposed sex, his body took over for his stunted mind. He didn't take it slow this time, instead licking straight up between the folds. Her moan reverberated loudly, and Zimyn knew the other guards must have heard. Damn them all.

She wasn't holding anything back as she rocked her hips against his mouth, seeking the friction she needed to get off—and he loved it. Every brush of his tongue left him hungry for more. This singular taste would never be enough.

Her breaths became shorter as he pumped in one digit, then two into her soaking core, his tongue continuing its ministrations of her clit.

"Please," she said as she yanked his hair. "At least take off your shirt so I have something good to look at."

Zimyn chuckled against her. He almost felt sorry for making her wait this long, but not sorry enough. He backed up slowly, unbuttoning his shirt and unbuckling his pants. She lifted herself onto her elbows, watching him attentively as his cock sprung free, beads of moisture already leaking from the tip.

"Is this what you need?" He said as he pumped himself.

"Don't be cocky now. I want to orgasm, not feed your ego. I have two perfectly good hands if you're incapable." As if proving it, she began to reach, but he lunged before she could.

"You've always been so impatient for things."

"A perk of being Queen."

Without a warning, he drove his cock into her, and she screamed. Now he could guarantee that the others heard them, but he still didn't care. She was blessedly tight as each inch of him drove deeper and deeper. As he kept thrusting, she tightened around him even more, until she finally exploded around him. He didn't stop. He wanted to pleasure her until tears filled her eyes, until she became so sensitive that she begged him to stop.

Ludelle grasped the sheets tightly, her eyes shut. He loved watching her like this. Completely unleashed, but also completely trusting him.

"I'm so close," she choked out.

He just grunted as he rocked in and out, his pace changing from fast to slow. Right when he hit a spot that had her moaning non-stop, he continued his rhythm until she screamed out again, his own body pleading to unleash itself.

He was so lost in his own lust-filled brain, he wasn't ready as she wrapped her legs around him and rolled them over until she was on top.

"It's my turn now."

She began bouncing, her breasts moving with her as she worked him. She used her ice power to freeze his wrists to the headboard, so he was completely at her mercy. Then she created small cubes of ice and placed them on his nipples. He winced, but the pain mixed with the pleasure of watching her take what she needed from him was so disorientating and magical. He only lasted a few more seconds before he yelled out. Moments later she followed, her body going limp as she braced her hands on his chest.

They were both trying to catch their breath. Ludelle's forehead was lined with sweat, her hair ruffled as her updo from earlier had fallen loose. As she removed herself from on top of him, and she hissed as his release trickled down her thighs.

"That was—" he started, but she placed a finger to his lips and shushed him.

He got it. He wanted to revel in this moment, too. Two satiated bodies. He broke out of his melted icy restraints and drew her in close, kissing the nape of her neck as she wrapped her body around his. At least they had this night. One he would never forget. One that would forever remain filled with the joy of their connection.

Fourteen

They had fallen asleep. Ludelle woke up in darkness, with Zimyn's arm curled around her waist tightly; his naked body fitted behind her own. She took a deep breath of him. The familiar scent eased her. Only this man would have the power to shatter her until she was weightless and piece her back together until she felt whole again in a matter of minutes.

She blinked away the tears that burned. This was all they had, and she savored him.

Zimyn moved, and she knew he was awake too when he kissed her shoulder gently.

She adjusted herself so that she faced him. "We fell asleep."

His gentle smile didn't look sorry. "We did."

She trailed her sharp claws down his chest, his muscles flexing as she scored his skin. She loved having this effect on him.

"How did it feel when you were crowned?"

Ludelle pushed herself back, stunned by the sudden question. She thought about it, though. When Balvan told her the news of her parents passing, she didn't register the words immediately. It had sounded like she was under water so they didn't penetrate fully. Then, she walked away and slammed her door for privacy. Kotyn had sensed the storm of emotions because she had rushed to her side to comfort Ludelle.

"I felt relieved."

Zimyn didn't say anything, letting her get her words out.

"My whole life was leading to that exact moment. It could happen any day, and all that anxious waiting had built up. When it finally happened, I was glad I could just do what I was meant to do. Does that make sense?"

His soft eyes took her in. "Completely."

She was so glad to have had him, to have someone who understood her so deeply like he did. It would hurt to watch him leave her. She kissed him deeply, and he responded to her immediately. Fervent touches turned to more, and he took his time with her, even while their time was running short. They finished with her laying on his chest, their legs tangled together.

What would life be like without him? When she first heard the news of his plans to leave, she thought she would be lonely. Now though, she would rely on her ladies in waiting. Any moment she wanted to crumble up, she would go to them. They could never truly replace Zimyn, but they could give her something close.

"Zimyn," she said against his hard chest. "I'm going to miss you so much."

He kissed her cheek, "Me too."

"Will you forget me?" she asked.

"Never," he responded, his morning-voice raspy.

Then she asked the question she had been the most afraid of hearing the answer to. "Was I not enough for you?"

He stiffened beneath her. "That's not fair."

"We could have been together." She knew she was pushing it, but she didn't care. He would be gone either way.

He pushed off the bed, shoving his feet into his pants, only stopping when he couldn't find his shirt. She pointed to the corner. "I have been haunted by you since the moment I laid my eyes on you." He exhaled sharply, thumbing a tight fist over his heart as if he wanted to rip through his flesh. "The moment I met you, I knew you would change the trajectory of my heart forever. You sealed it when you came running straight at me, even at your parents' chagrin, and showed me your powers that you were so excited about and stated that one day you would be Queen. I knew then that you were different. That being Queen was not a burden you dreaded but one you wanted to prove you deserved. And I loved that about you because I felt the same way about becoming Captain."

Ludelle began crying but she didn't wipe the tears away. "So have me," her voice wavered, with this one last plea. "I'm all yours."

He shook his head. "But I wouldn't be. I would be your secret, and we both deserve better than that." He cleared his throat. He was now fully clothed as Ludelle laid bare, only their once shared sheets providing her protection. "I'm leaving. I will not be your shadow. I will not allow people to dismiss your excellence by standing in your way."

Ludelle's heart shattered as Zimyn stepped out the door.

Zimyn thanked the Weather Gods that the halls were empty, save for a few guards standing watch, who were easy enough to avoid since he knew exactly where they were stationed. Growing up, he had loved the night shift. The quiet nights allowed him time to think without the worry of guests getting lost or the pressure of having to appear perfect at all times. He could relax his shoulders, a simple luxury. On lucky nights, Ludelle would visit him. She would sit on the opposite side of the wall with books or correspondences to read up on, or she would try to find ways to distract him, many times that consisted of throwing small icicles at his legs. But how could she never realize that just her presence would always be a distraction?

Now, he felt disassociated from himself, his body and mind two separate beings as if he had too much to drink.

He reprimanded himself for being so damn weak. They had been so close to her Undertaking. He knew having her completely would have made it harder for him to go, and it did. Stepping off the mattress had been like ripping off a limb.

He didn't even know where he was headed. Perhaps he should shake off some of the anger before he tried interacting with anyone. Or he could go to his father and throw another ice figurine at the wall.

Rolling his neck, he decided on the training rings. He wouldn't disrupt his father's peace again.

He walked down and far, on the opposite side of the castle. It was a quieter area, since guests hardly went there. As he did, he noticed a trail of red.

He turned the corner and bumped straight into someone. Disoriented, Zimyn grabbed the person's shoulders to steady them. Before he could fully comprehend what was happening, a shooting pain exploded on his thigh. He fell to his knees as it spread across his whole leg, no longer able to carry the weight of his body anymore.

He saw black right as Balvan's face loomed out of the shadows.

"I knew you would always make things harder for me." It was the last thing Zimyn heard before his head hit the ground.

When Zimyn came to, his head throbbed unbearingly. He had no clue where he was, only that it was dark and that his body ached from having been lying on a hard surface. His hands were tied, and he didn't bother struggling. He relented himself to this.

Memories of the past few hours flashed behind his eyes. His solitude, Ludelle and him in bed together, his frustrations with himself.

"Good, you're awake." Balvan said as he walked in, the light from the hallway spilling through before the door shut again. Balvan held a lantern that barely illuminated anything, but Zimyn could just make out the outline of a desk and a bookshelf.

His study, then. Zimyn had never been inside it before, having been told it was strictly forbidden. His father had been very stern about that fact, so even as a child, Zimyn took no chances.

"We only have a short time."

Zimyn knew that Balvan purposefully piqued his curiosity, and he despised that he so easily gave in. "Short time until what?"

"Glad you asked," he responded cheerily. "The Undertaking. You and I will be participating."

"I don't understand." How could they be participating? Only Ludelle and her future betrothed were supposed to be involved.

"Ludelle's Undertaking is a unique one." Balvan sat at his desk, resting his crossed heels on it. The dim light only allowed Zimyn to see the one side of his face clearly. "She has always been conflicted between the responsibility of her Court and her affection towards you."

"So what, she's going to be forced to pick between me and a noble?"

"Not anymore," he said exasperated.

That was when Zimyn noticed the unmoving body. Lord Cirrus lay there, his neck at an awkward angle and red bloomed against his chest.

"What—"

"Lord Cirrus wanted you dead, especially when he heard that Ludelle was in your room. I stopped him."

Zimyn shook his head confused. "Why? Why did you stop him?" Zimyn thought Balvan would be overjoyed if the advisor found the Queen's Captain dead.

"Because a Queen in mourning would not be productive to this court." Balvan didn't let Zimyn get another word in. "The dream about the Undertaking came to Sveta a few months ago. She would have been forced to pick between you and Cirrus, until he tried ruining that." Balavan nodded his head towards the dead body. "Sveta had a new dream last night. Ludelle will be picking between you and me."

"Is that why you hated him? Why you pushed Ludelle away from him?"

"I pushed him away because I wanted his place."

Zimyn scoffed. Of course he would want to be by Ludelle's side. "Even if she picks you, you would only be her consort. You would have no actual power."

"Maybe not at first, but ice is so fragile. Easily broken."

Zimyn tried untying the damn knots of his binds, but he only accomplished making his skin raw. "Then just throw yourself into the Undertaking. Why give her the second option?"

"I don't know the will of the Gods. Perhaps, the people need to see where her loyalties lie. She'll hesitate when she learns. This is, of course, if you dare to enter with me. Perhaps, you'd prefer to wipe your hands of all this madness and leave immediately on your travels. Why sacrifice yourself to an unknown?"

Zimyn shook his head. "I have to enter."

"And why's that?"

"So she can prove to everyone that she'll alway make the right choice. She'll pick you and the court."

Balvan shrugged, unconvinced. "We will see."

Fifteen

"Y ou're late," Sveta said.

Ludelle waved her off, stepping into the small divine temple room. Although windows of shattered and reformed ice that formed a mosaic lined the walls, no sun peeked through. Candles of cold flame were the only source of light. A sanctuary of memorial. "A Queen is never late. Everyone else is just early."

Ludelle had to beg one of the guards to call a maid for her in Zimyn's room so that she could bring Ludelle some fresh clothes. It was embarrassing, but Ludelle refused to be caught wearing the same clothes as the night before, especially with the way Zimyn had left her naked and alone on his bed. She made sure to give them enough coin to keep quiet.

"Even the Weather Gods?" Sveta slammed her prayer book closed and rose from kneeling. Her white and silver robes swished behind her. "I would think you would not want to anger them the night before your first Undertaking."

Ludelle winced. "I suppose not."

"You haven't matured much since your young days. Still no respect for the Gods that made you who you are." The minister honed her gaze downwards. "I see you also still play with your hands when you get uncomfortable."

Ludelle hid them behind her back. "I would like to get this over with. I need as much rest as possible for tomorrow."

"You need much more than rest. You need the Gods." Sveta opened up a small glass cabinet that housed many trinkets that Ludelle had never paid much attention to. "And you need me."

Before Ludelle could speak, Sveta revealed the small object in her hands. The sapphires that covered the object glimmered. Sveta opened it.

"A mirror?" Ludelle asked flatly. "That is not impressive, nor very helpful."

Sveta sighed. "It's more than just a mirror. It's a heart. The Heart of the court."

Now that she pointed it out, the shape did resemble a heart. "Each ruler of the Snow Court has their own Heart to save and protect during their Undertakings. Not only are you tasked to survive and come out the other side with your consort, but you cannot let this break."

"What happens if I do?"

"I see your curiosity hasn't waned either..." Sveta gave her a sideward glance. "This holds the power of the court. As the year progresses, the powers that you use are fused into this." Her steady hands unclasped something inside the compact mirror. "And this small sapphire glows." She picked it out. It looked no different from the sapphires that were mined, the ones that decorated the castle. But it glowed, pulsed. "If it breaks, the power goes straight back to the Weather Gods, and they will curse the land as infertile. Then, we'd all die."

"No pressure," Ludelle quipped under her breath.

"Your first task will be to find the Heart, then you will wear this around your neck during the rest of your Undertaking as you save your consort. The people trust that you will do whatever it takes to keep it safe."

Ludelle swiped the mirror from the minister's hands. "That is obvious."

"Then, I wish you luck Queen Ludelle. Please take some time to pray to the Weather Gods, submit your choice for consort. They're waiting. Just like we are waiting to see you save this court."

Without another sinister word, Sveta left.

"You looked about as excited as I did when I found out that my cousin was Queen," Helena said as she dined on the fruit tray that was meant for Ludelle. "Which is to say, not at all." She pouted as she missed her mouth and the berry rolled from Ludelle's clean bed to the floor. Kotyn pounced for it.

"I am an hour away from my Undertaking. I think I deserve to be a little bit moody."

"You're always moody, though," she said cheekily, as she burrowed herself further into the pillows.

Ludelle rolled her eyes, but sighed at her reflection in the mirror. Her whole entourage of ladies in waiting woke her up, helped her dress into her fighting leathers, and provided words of comfort. Now, only Ludelle's cousin remained.

"My conversation with Sveta last night just rattled me a bit," Ludelle said honestly, though it was not just that. She wasn't expecting another element to this Undertaking, another thing to worry about as she fought for her life.

After Sveta left, Ludelle kneeled down and prayed, even though she hated doing it. She asked for a safe Undertaking and that they guided her through whatever test she would face and who her consort should be. She knew who the smart choice was. The one the people would applaud her for making because he was part of a family that helped the court prosper. The sapphire hidden in the mirror only confirmed that. A sign from the Gods that she needed, she supposed.

Twirling around a spoon from her breakfast, Ludelle inspected her own gaunt face. She slept horribly, unsurprisingly. Zimyn's parting words to her replayed in her head over and over again.

Helena came up behind her and grabbed her shoulders. "You've prepared for this all your life. You have nothing to worry about."

Ludelle snorted. "That is easy for you to say. You will be comfortably drinking warm cider while wrapped in furs." Ludelle raised a brow. "Or perhaps Villeta."

Helena ducked her head, but a blush stained her cheeks. "Maybe."

Ludelle's face turned serious as she faced her cousin and lifted her chin. "I am happy that you will be happy."

"I think I'm owed it after having to deal with your pining for years."

Scoffing, Ludelle playfully slapped her arm, doing her best to stop the stinging in her eyes. "Yes, well someone deserves for all that pining to turn into something good. I am truly sorry for not noticing it sooner. It was right in front of me, and I allowed my own troubles to get in the way."

"Can't blame you, really. If I found men attractive, then I wouldn't have been able to keep my eyes off him either." They both chuckled. "I should go before you're called."

Ludelle nodded, grateful that at least these last moments could be filled with light. It would serve as a reminder of what awaited her after she survived the hardest challenge she would face in her life.

Sixteen

Ludelle followed Balvan and Sveta up the mountain, her legs already starting to ache, which she didn't think to be fair. She should be starting with full energy. Though maybe it was a sign that her Undertaking would be less physically demanding. Knowing the Weather Gods, she didn't hold out hope.

Balvan and Sveta were side by side, exchanging a few quiet words as Ludelle looked at the back of their heads wondering what it would be like to smash them together and run away from all this with Zimyn. Ludelle almost gasped at her outrageous thoughts. Never in her life did she actually consider shirking her role before. The nerves must be getting to her.

She also had the realization that she never had seen Balvan and Sveta in the same room before, much less having a conversation. It was strange, if Ludelle was being honest. She didn't like it, the two of them conspiring together as she walked to her Undertaking. Shouldn't they be offering her words of advice?

"We're almost there," Balvan yelled over the roaring wind, the climate only getting worse as they reached higher altitudes. At least her fighting leathers were lined with fur.

Sveta gave her a nervous glance, the bottom of her robes soaked in dirt.

They reached the mountain caves, and Ludelle could hear the crowd inside. Her people would be waiting for her as she completed her Undertaking, excited for another year of prosperity and power. Ludelle gulped down her doubts of not delivering.

"I must go," Balvan announced ceremoniously, as if Ludelle cared where he was. "I have a few matters to attend to before you start."

They both nodded, watching him go and getting lost in the people.

Ludelle surveyed the crowd for a familiar face—hating that she did. Of course he wouldn't show. Zimyn was likely packing up his things, passing on his duties to whoever would be taking over for him.

"Don't get distracted now," Sveta reprimanded. "He's not here. And you look like a hungry child desperate for milk with the way you're craning your neck."

If Ludelle weren't moments away from her Undertaking, those words would be enough to send Sveta to the dungeons. Once Ludelle came out of this, she needed to find a way to scold her lack of respect.

"Who says I am looking for him?" She would never be more grateful than she was now to see Zimyn's father. "I wanted to speak with our former Captain and ask if he had any words of comfort since he spent a lot of time with my father to prepare for his Undertakings."

Sveta didn't seem impressed, but she scurried off, giving them both some privacy to chat.

The man's face, one that looked so much like Zimyn's with the same colored eyes and whose arms showed scars of where his scales once rested, seemed wary, as if he was hesitant to speak with her. Strange, since he had no issue reprimanding both his son and her when they acted out as children. Sometimes, he acted more like a parent to her than her own ever did.

"Say it," she said, tapping her feet against the cold stone. Her surroundings left little for comfort, and she tried guessing what her Undertaking would involve.

His eyes drifted behind her, getting lost into his own head. "Your father always had a ritual before his Undertakings."

"Yes I know. We all go to pray to the Gods for luck." Since it was her first Undertaking, Ludelle also submitted Lord Cirrus' name for her consort, so he would be on the other side of all this for her.

"Not that," he shook his head. The crowd began to situate themselves into clusters. Her time was running out, and she didn't care about hearing about her father. "He wrote letters, ones he would hand to me for safekeeping in case things didn't go well. I never read them nor did anyone else, as he would have me burn them in the cold flames after he survived, but they were addressed to his wife, to Balvan, to you of course, to me even, and surprisingly, to Zimyn. I never knew why my son was included, since I know your father did everything in his power to keep you two apart." Ludelle snorted. That was an understatement. One time, he locked them in separate rooms after they were caught stealing from the kitchen. Well, Zimyn was stealing some chocolate cake on her behalf, but he took the blame with her. "I would like to think he ultimately had a soft spot for Zimyn, that even he understood that he would ensure you were safe on the throne."

"My father was too shortsighted to even consider Zimyn's importance in my life."

"Maybe so," he agreed. "Maybe we all are a bit shortsighted; we see only one way to things when there are various options to consider."

Ludelle stopped him before he could continue spouting unhelpful nonsense. "So why tell me all this?"

"Because your father, like you, worried about the crown and his court, but also cared for the people in his everyday life, too. And he stood right before his Undertaking, scared that he would lose it all."

"Well, he did lose it all," Ludelle said, crossing her arms. "He died in vain on that stupid trip to the Solar Continent, dragging my mother with him." Ludelle had tried so hard to convince him to let one of them stay in case something went awry. Even if her mother was only consort, having both members of royalty on one ship at the same time would only lead to trouble. Her father saw that it was the only way to convince the Solar King of a potential trade alliance.

"They died together because they knew that was the only way to go."

"My mother and father were not in love. They had their fair share of people they bedded."

"Oh yes, I know." He laughed, his strong chest rising and falling. "I have walked in on them many times." Ludelle internally gagged thinking about her parents in such a way. "It doesn't mean there was no love. After all, your father's Undertaking tested that love. Like I said, he had choices, and he always picked the one where your mother came back on the other side with him." Seeing her annoyed face, he sighed. "I'm not saying he was a good man, or a good father, but he wasn't entirely a villain either. I think your grandmother had a large role in that. She cared for Zimyn deeply."

Before Ludelle could ask any further questions, Zimyn's father walked away, leaving her with a cryptic message that confused her entirely. She had no idea her grandmother had a soft spot for Zimyn. Now, she might never know the full details.

Ludelle had assumed that the goal of her father's Undertaking had always been to save her mother from the creature, like she was some damsel. Ludelle supposed her father also had the Heart of the court that required protecting, too. Could her father have been faced with the opportunity to pick only his crown over his wife? If so, Ludelle was shocked that he never left her mother to die, to be eaten up by the haunting monster.

And if that was the case, what did that mean once Ludelle entered her own Undertaking? She needed a consort, so what choices would she be offered?

Seventeen

Sveta guided Ludelle to her starting point. She anxiously pulled at her braid, her claws getting caught in it and ripping a chunk from her scalp. She let the wind carry the strands, like seeds feeding the earth.

Sveta said, "Once the horn blasts, you'll make your way through this tunnel and your Undertaking will begin." The minister blessed Ludelle as she created symbols of the court with her thumb on Ludelle's forehead. "May the Weather Gods bless you. May the Snow Court continue to thrive."

Ludelle took in the words and allowed them to coat her skin like a film of ice. She spared one final glance to all those behind her, each of them with hopeful eyes. She wished she could stare into Zimyn's one last time, but apparently, Queens did *not* always get what they wanted.

Ludelle rolled her shoulders. She wielded no weapons and was stripped of her powers of ice. It was just her and whatever awaited on the other side.

She could do this.

She had no other choice.

The horn's blast reverberated against the cavernous walls, and Ludelle ventured inside the small tunnel. She had to shrink her body and turn it sideways at points just to be able to get through, but she could feel cold, fresh air. This high up, Ludelle didn't stall to discover what she had to face.

When she pushed her body out of the tunnel, it was both worse and better than she expected.

Large walls of ice formed a labyrinth so tall that Ludelle couldn't see anything beyond it. It was eerily quiet, as if its height swallowed all sound. Even the wind from earlier couldn't penetrate through. A shield from the elements maybe, but already she felt the world closing in on her.

Ludelle took a deep breath. At least it didn't seem like she would need to fight against anything. It would just be her and her mind as she weaved through and found the Heart, and then her betrothed. Simple, she convinced herself.

Ludelle stepped forward and almost slipped on the icy floor, her arms making circles to gain her balance. She scrunched her brows, confused. Her home had floors made of ice and never before had she struggled with it. Could it be due to her powers being gone? She didn't let that deter her from what she needed to accomplish. She moved forward, concentrating on taking it slow.

At the first fork in her path, she chose left. Most people would pick the right, their dominant side, she thought, so the less obvious choice made sense, and she didn't question it beyond that. She worked her way through more paths, coming at some dead ends and digging her heels into the ice to mark where she'd already been.

The experience was dizzying. She had no idea how big this maze could be but she assumed the Heart would be at the center of it. The clouded skies provided her no comfort, as her heart leapt at every turn expecting something to jump at her, to dig its claws into her flesh. The unknown of it all was unnerving.

It was much easier to practice for the Undertaking than be in it. In her training sessions, she knew that she would come out of it alive. Here, the reality of it all made it hard to even think strategically. She had played card games with opponents so well their minds had spun, untied herself from mischievous knots that Zimyn made, yet it had all come to nothing now.

But Ludelle trudged on, her doubts bubbling up even more when she ended up back to where she started. Right at the beginning...*fuck*.

The tunnel back to the cave seemed like a warm embrace in comparison to going back into the labyrinth. How would her people react if she just walked back in—no Heart, no consort? The horror of it was enough to have Ludelle turn back around, even if she didn't want to start over again. She recognized the test for what it was: a mental game. One she specifically asked the Gods for, so she didn't take that blessing lightly. Nothing would come easily for her here, she had no one else to call for help. It was just her and her thoughts against herself.

She grumbled but smacked her own cheek to reorient her focus. Ludelle was greeted by only a thin layer of ice underneath her feet as she stepped back in. She heard a crack under her, so she lifted her foot back to the tunnel entryway.

She gazed down at the wet ice. It was melting. That's why she was slipping around. The castle never melted, the ice strong and intact. It would have been too easy to just let Ludelle wander aimlessly.

Not only did she need to find the Heart, protect it as she found Cirrus, and get out, she was being timed, too. The Weather Gods were not on her side, then. A smart way to humble her it seemed, so she gave the skies a middle finger—because it couldn't get worse—and entered again.

She dug her claws into the wall as she braced herself, her arms outstretched and her feet gliding across the slick ice. It was beginning to thin out faster now, so much so, she could just make out the large expanse of space between her and her doom if she didn't hurry. It was so high that she knew she would never survive it. Cirrus would also die.

All her markings from earlier had melted so she had no clue where she had already been. Frustrated and desperate, Ludelle took a dangerous second to think of how to best track her movements now. She could feel herself sinking down. Sweat beaded along her brow. Ludelle looked up and the clouds moved quickly, the barest hints of the sun coming through.

She didn't think twice as she sliced across her palm and let some of her blue blood flow on the ground. The small pool of blood caused the ice to melt slightly, but she had no other choice.

She made fewer mistakes this time, perhaps the added pressure boosted her instincts. She didn't complain either way.

Thinking back on her conversation with Zimyn's father, Ludelle wondered how nervous her father and her grandmother had been during their Undertakings. Did they walk in confidently? Did each Undertaking get harder or easier as they became more familiar with the test?

The biggest question Ludelle had: Why did the Gods hold their powers hostage and force them to partake in an Undertaking? If they were all-giving and actually cared, surely they would gladly fuel the land they ruled so the people below would prosper.

Right now, she had more pressing matters to worry about, like the fact that the thin layer of ice would not be able to bear her weight soon. She didn't know how much longer she had, but she begged whoever would listen that she would make it to the Heart soon.

Her nails ached with how much they were holding her upright, and before she knew what was happening, she crashed to her knees. The ice underneath her splintered and fell. She quickly reached out and clawed the wall, but the sharp ice scraped her face as she did. She would leave this maze bruised and cut, if she didn't die first. She hung there, her legs dangling as she held on, but she couldn't hold on forever. The distance below daunted her. The fall would last too long for comfort, with too much time to think before her body splattered against the rocks and trees.

It couldn't end like this. Not without saying goodbye to Zimyn. That thought had her gritting her teeth and swinging her legs until she could toss herself back up onto the maze. A few of her nails cracked and broke in the process, but she could care less now that she was back on somewhat solid ground. She stayed there, heavy-breathing, scared—but she couldn't stop now.

She decided to crawl to keep moving at least, even if at a much slower pace. Ahead of her was a long straight path and then a left turn. Ludelle prayed that this would be it. If it wasn't, then her body might actually fail her.

She sobbed in relief when a large clearing revealed itself. At the center, on a glimmering pedestal of ice stood the Heart of the Snow Court.

She didn't hesitate as she ran and grabbed it, the cold exterior biting into her skin. She sagged in relief. One task accomplished. Now, she just had to find Cirrus and get back to the caves. Right as she stepped off the platform to start the next phase, the ground shook beneath her and the side of the maze she just solved crumbled and fell.

Eighteen

L udelle blinked in disbelief at the sight before her. She hadn't realized how far she had walked from the starting point. The distance between her and the tunnel was stark and wide, a looming presence. At least she now knew that Cirrus waited for her on the other side of the maze. Less options meant she could go faster.

She put the compact over her neck and tucked it into her leathers, giving it extra protection in case she decided it would be fun to fall again. She didn't want a stupid mistake to be the reason her court fell.

There were two points of entry back into the veins of the maze. She picked left, and she could have sworn she felt the Heart of the court thud against her skin. Hopefully, a good sign.

The ground beneath her hadn't started melting yet, giving her more traction to walk faster, but sharp icicles poked out of the walls, some long enough that she had to adjust and dodge.

This time, Ludelle purposefully hit every path possible, even the dead ends, making her blood more important than ever. Cirrus could be waiting for her in any corner, and she didn't want to miss him.

An icicle shot out of nowhere, stabbing Ludelle in the shoulder. She screamed in pain, pulling it out of her and holding the wound. She heaved as she looked at her ripped clothes and the small hole that was bleeding out, luckily not too deep. She didn't let it deter her, she kept moving. The faster she could get out, the faster she could call the healer. She just made sure to be careful as she continued.

Now that she had the Heart, her confidence had risen. She could do this. She would find Cirrus, get the hell out, and tell Zimyn goodbye. Tell him her heart beat just for him and that no consort would ever compare. She would dream of *his* hands on her at night.

She would also tell him that she was happy for him because he deserved to see the world. Just like her, he had been locked into the Snow Court his whole life, only leaving on official court business, which were rare to begin with and never allowed time for actual exploration of the destination. Now, he would have that freedom he clearly desired, even if it was without her.

She didn't stop. Not even a moment to think through her actions. She made a sharp turn and gasped at the sight around the corner. It was Cirrus!

But as he lay there, a red spot bloomed on his chest. Ludelle covered her mouth as a cry escaped her lips.

Was she too late? Had the Weather Gods cursed her to a worse fate?

"Ludelle," a whimper called out. The sound, weak, but with it being so silent, she could easily hear it. "Lud—" Her body froze as she recognized who it belonged to. It couldn't be.

She ran.

She slammed into a wall, her face hitting it so hard she had to blink away the white dots in her vision. She would bruise, but she didn't care. She didn't care about anything except for the other bleeding body that lay there. Zimyn, whose hands and legs were tied and whose eyes were closed, opened his mouth to call out to her again. He was caged in by a myriad of icicles. She tore through them with her hands quickly to reach him, the sharp ends slicing through her skin.

She dropped to her knees at his side and placed her hand on his cheek. "Shh. I'm here." She wiped his wet hair away from his face and revealed all the bruising. His scales had been ripped off, his arms coated in blood where they once were.

"What happened?" She whispered frantically, doing her best to tamp down the devastation and fear. Water began to pool beneath them, the ice melting at a quicker pace with the two of them on it, but she shakily undid the knots that restrained him.

Zimyn moved—or tried to—but he could barely hold his weight. His arms strained as he lifted his torso up so that he could lean against the wall behind him. She wanted to push him back down but was scared that if she pressed too hard he wouldn't get up again.

His eyes were closed, exhausted from all the pain. Ludelle just noticed his right hand, how the bones sat awkwardly. She reached out, but he flinched away.

"Who did this to you?" Whoever did would feel her wrath. She would cut every inch of their body, watch them bleed, and freeze their dead body as a display.

"You," he started, but took a deep breath before continuing. "Go away."

"I'm not leaving you," she said adamantly. If he thought that she would leave him in this state, then he didn't know her at all. Her stiff knees crawled closer to him. "Tell me what happened."

His head rolled towards her. "Win the Undertaking, Ludelle."

"But—" She was so confused. Why was he even here? It was supposed to be Cirrus. No one prepared her for this.

"Balvan."

"Did he do this?"

Zimyn jerked his head. "He's here," Zimyn managed to say, his eyes fluttering shut again. "Find him and get out."

She cupped Zimyn's face. "I don't understand."

Zimyn winced, as he cradled his broken hand in his lap.

Ludelle worked to piece it all together. Balvan was here somewhere, and he had hurt Zimyn, unforgivably. Yet Zimyn wanted her to find him, to survive the Undertaking with him on his side. Meaning Balvan would become her consort. That couldn't be...

Advisors could never rule because there needed to be a separation. Balvan provided her his objective advice on matters, but he couldn't do that if he were her consort. It would be an obvious conflict of interest.

And she couldn't just abandon Zimyn now! The ground below him would soon splinter wide open and he would fall to his death

Was this the choice Zimyn's father had spoken of?

If so, he was wrong.

A cornered choice wasn't a choice at all.

Zimyn could barely feel anything. His body had become so cold and so tired, that only numbness consumed him. Even his broken hand just added weight to his suffering. Balvan had laughed as he took a large chunk of solid ice and bashed it against his dominant hand, knowing that no matter what, Zimyn could never return to his role as Captain if it wasn't healed in time.

As Balvan dragged his body through the maze, Zimyn had accepted his fate. If he died, then Ludelle could finally let him go and rule in peace. If he lived, they both would come to the same conclusion that he no longer would be suited for the job and that leaving was the best option. It was a sense of peace that he'd only felt once before—in that quiet moment where they both lied together after their joining.

Now though, he was in a living nightmare. He had pleaded with the Gods that Ludelle wouldn't stumble across him, that she would just find Balvan and reluctantly accept him as her consort. She would hate it with every fiber of her being, but she would do it. Which is why she needed to abandon him and continue with her Undertaking.

Bracing himself, Zimyn struggled to his knees. Ludelle wrapped her arm around his waist as she helped him, but she didn't let go once he got to his feet. She held on tightly, and he savored it. The way she fit perfectly against him.

His blood marred her skin. Even then, she was the most beautiful thing he had ever laid his eyes on. Her determination and bravery, even now, pierced him. Every drop of blood was for her: for her title and her honor.

"Go," he stammered out.

She shook her head against his neck. "I can't leave you."

"You have to."

Warm tears dropped onto his skin, and the sensation both broke him and anchored him to this moment as his breaths became more labored, as his body prepared to shut down. The one last thing he would do was convince her that she needed to let him go. It would be the greatest privilege of his life.

"It all depends on this. Don't waste it on me."

She peeked her eyes up at him. "Don't say that. Every second I had with you was the most special. The rest of it never mattered."

"But it did, Ludelle. It got you this far. Now you need to go." He brushed a stray tear from under her eye. "Let my life mean something. Let it all have been for you." He pushed something into her hands. She gasped as she saw the ring—his mother's. She knew what it meant to him.

She shuddered as she slipped it onto her finger. It fit perfectly. "I will never forget you." Then, she leaned forward, pressing her lips against his cold ones. He would spend his whole afterlife dreaming of the heat of her. The Gods would never hear the end of how special this woman was.

She let go of him, but it was like pulling teeth to get them apart. Their souls had always been entwined, but they needed to be severed forever now.

"I love you," she said as the last of them separated.

"I love you," he said as he closed his eyes, releasing her do what always had to be done.

Nineteen

Ludelle could barely carry herself as she went. But she did. Because if she really had a choice, then her choice was ripping Balvan's heart out. He would not survive. Whatever trick he thought he had figured out would fail. She would make sure of it.

All the trust that she and her ancestors had placed on such a role had been obliterated in a blink. If she made it out of this alive, she would make sure that no more celebrations would be held in honor of the advisors. They would work *for* her, not with her anymore.

She swiped back her hair, not realizing that she had Zimyn's blood all over her hands— the crimson staining her bone-white palms. She didn't care that she looked savage and unwieldy, the opposite of the picture-perfect Queen she aimed to be. Let the Weather Gods look down on her and know that she fought hard for this, and that she wasn't yet done. She would tear this whole test down for hurting the one person that she wanted to protect.

The Heart slowed its thudding as she got further away from Zimyn, or hopefully, closer to Balvan.

Her anger almost made her miss the noise that sounded from behind her. A cough. One she knew too well. One she would guarantee she would never hear again.

Ludelle creeped slowly as she popped her head on the other side to see if she was correct. Balvan was leaning casually against the wall, bored and not a scratch on him, as he inspected his nails. He was out of his usual formal garb and in his own set of fighting leathers. Ludelle had never realized how toned he was under all those baggier clothes, that even in his older age, he clearly still trained.

Before she could throw herself at him and end his life, he said casually, "It's not what you think."

She scoffed. "What else am I supposed to think? Cirrus is dead and Zimyn is seconds away from it."

He stepped towards her, but he couldn't get very far—as if phantom hands held him back. He couldn't touch her. Not until she decided that she wanted him to. That revelation was the most freeing moment of her life because what everyone had told her was true: ultimately, the choice was hers. This entire maze was full of choices. Now she needed to end it.

"You have always been so blinded by your own needs and wants."

She narrowed her eyes as she stepped closer and closer, one foot slowly in front of the other. He didn't look scared, just resigned to his fate. Almost as if he were ready for it.

"Tell. Me. The. Truth," she bit out, her claws now out and ready to strike. "Why are you here?"

He slid down the icy wall and sat down. "So you can have your love, and I can find my way back to mine."

Ludelle stopped, the fog of bloodlust dissipated. "What do you mean?" she gritted out. The lack of clear explanation grinded on her bones.

"Zimyn believes that I want to be your consort. Let him. I taunted him to think that I was the villain here so that he would agree to enter. Don't tell him that I wanted to die here, that I killed Cirrus for my own personal revenge, but also so that I could replace him." At her stunned silence, he continued, "You can have Zimyn. He'll believe you killed me in his honor and he would forgive you for it. He would stay as your consort forever. I will die and go back to Olana."

"My grandmother?" Her shoulders slackened as the reality of what he was saying was hitting her.

He nodded, his eyes watering now. "I loved her and she loved me, but we could never be together, not with me as her advisor."

Ludelle didn't believe him. "That cannot be."

"I'm not here so you can question our love," he snapped and his voice echoed around the frosty chamber. "I'm here so you can have yours. Take it or not, but time is running out."

"What revenge?" she asked.

"Pardon?"

"What personal revenge led you to kill Cirrus?"

Balvan's jaw tensed, as if lost in a memory that angered him. "Your grandfather once tried to overthrow Olana. He made a deal with Cirrus' own grandfather—they came to some kind of agreement that would benefit the court. It forced your grandmother to step down from her position prematurely. Cirrus' family is not a good one, and Olana made me promise to keep you away from them."

It all made sense now, why Balvan pushed her away from Lord Cirrus, why he would rather her marry Zimyn over the Lord, even if it wasn't the strategic match.

"Your grandmother always knew that Zimyn made you happy, and she always hoped you could be together. I told her it was the wrong direction, but she was insistent that you'd both change the court for the better. I never aimed to fulfill that wish for her, but events unfolded that way." He shrugged, but turned stern. "Now, make your choice."

Could she trap Zimyn in a marriage that he had been ready to run from to find his own happiness? It would be cruel to lie to him forever, but she couldn't marry Balvan.

And in the end, Ludelle and Zimyn loved each other deeply. As Balvan had said, Zimyn would accept this destiny happily in time. He could give up his role as Captain and still travel when he pleased. She would tell the people she had no other option but to choose him, that the Weather Gods blessed their union.

She looked at Balvan who stared at his feet. "Are you sure?"

He bent his head down lower, the only indication that he heard her.

"I thought I hated you."

"My duty has always been to serve you. You have a vision for the court, Ludelle. I would not have been part of it anyways. "

"Thank you," she whispered. "For all the years that you helped my family, and for this."

She didn't wait any longer before she went back to the man who earned her heart years ago.

Twenty

It didn't take long before she was back at Zimyn's side. She slammed to her knees, chipping some ice on the way, and cradled his head into her neck. His pallor had worsened already. Time was running short.

"Don't leave me." she whispered, brushing her fingers through his knotted and bloody hair. "Not yet. We'll leave together. I'll be yours for eternity."

He didn't respond at all, not even a groan came out of his lips.

"Zimyn, I need you to wake up. Just for a little longer, and I'll get you help. We just have to get out of here." She was ready to bow down to the Weather Gods and offer anything. "I don't know what else to do."

She held onto him for what could have been hours, trying to warm him up as she clutched him like a lifeline. She whispered into his ear to remind him of what waited for him if he woke up, if he came back to her, but it was too cold. He wouldn't make it. And everything she had done and would do as Queen wouldn't matter if he wasn't there beside her. He was her salvation, her balance, her love. Without him, she would crack under the pressure. The solid glacier that he helped form her into would break.

"Please," she begged, desperate for anyone to hear her. She pressed a soft kiss to his lips. They didn't respond to her, so she lay there holding him tightly. If this was his end, then at least he wouldn't die alone—though she did not have the courage to say goodbye. The words froze on her lips, refusing to budge.

Her legs had started to become numb and her back hurt, but she didn't let him go. She knew she needed to leave soon, without a consort, but at least she had the Heart. Her court would prosper for one more year. She just hoped the people would accept her as a lone royal. More importantly, how would the people feel about Balvan betraying her? Court advisors had been revered for years as trustworthy, always having the best interest of the court at their core. Would they blame her for leaving him? She would need to rethink how the court would function now, too.

The Heart of the court beat rapidly underneath her clothes, as if it wanted to burst out of its cage and leap towards the man that lay dying before her. Like it had a mind of its own.

She pulled it out and unclasped it to reveal the sapphire stone inside. A light blue aura beamed from it in flashes, beckoning her to touch it. She pressed a shaky finger to it and the light disappeared, swallowing back into the stone. Removing her finger, the light came back. She tried to make sense of it, what exactly the Heart was telling her...until it finally clicked.

The power was not meant for her. It was hers to *give*.

To give to her people and her land. To give to the one she loved.

It was a heart built to share.

She took the small gemstone out, holding it in her palm. It rolled and warmed, the sensation of it comforted her, reminding her of why she fought so hard. Perhaps it could do the same for Zimyn.

She dragged it across Zimyn's bleeding arm, and already the wounds began to heal as the sapphire continued to glow. His scales did not reform, but she would bestow them onto him again once they survived this. She kept going, letting it touch every bit of his bare skin that had been bruised and torn.

By the time she finished, he looked alive again. At least from the outside.

She tore open his shirt, revealing his broad but unmoving chest—one she had seen so many times full of life, while he trained, changed, and as he lay beneath her writhing body as she took her pleasure.

She had it memorized. Each scar, each mole, each hair. The armor that protected her favorite part of him. She pressed her palm at the center of it. Barely a flutter. His heart was weak while the one she held beat strongly. There was only one conclusion to this: if anyone deserved her heart, it was him. She forgot about all the consequences that would stem out of her decision because she didn't care. It was a sacrifice she was willing to make. She would rather spend her whole life proving herself as a competent leader than live any day without him.

Without hesitation, she slammed the sapphire into his chest. The stone sank through his skin and muscle and bone where it would be forever protected.

The world around them shook. Ludelle squeezed Zimyn's body, nervous that this would be it. "I love you," she whispered into his neck. But as they lay there weathering the storm, they did not fall. The other side of the maze, where Balvan was trapped, crumbled away. With all the commotion of the maze's implosion, she didn't even know if Balvan had screamed. She hoped it was quick. She hoped that her grandmother waited for him with outstretched arms.

Though Ludelle realized with a sinking horror that if they did not move, they would be the next to fall. Time was running out for them. The ground beneath them started to melt at a quicker pace as water pooled swiftly under their bodies.

Zimyn gasped, then, shooting up straight, a cloud of fog escaping his chapped lips. He coughed, tears pouring out of his eyes as he adjusted to all the raw power now running through him.

"What did you do?!" He sat there astonished and in disbelief, and it was the most wonderful moment of her life, so far.

"What I should have done long ago." Her heart had always belonged to him. Now, he would have it imbued into his very being forever.

"But what does that even mean?"

"It means," she said with a smile on her face. "That no one will dare harm or question you. You hold the power of the court within you."

He shook his head. "It can't be that simple," he countered. This whole situation hadn't been simple, though. Not for her. She faced every hurdle with doubt but overcame it because he waited on the other side. She would do it all over again for him.

When she didn't respond, he asked, "So you chose me?"

"Yes," she chuckled, grabbing his face and kissing him deeply. His tired arms took her waist as she wrapped her arms around his neck, but he hissed in pain. His right hand had not completely healed, it seemed. But it didn't matter, never to her.

"I'll choose you every time." She kissed his right cheek. "I promise that." Now, his left. "You'll be by my side forever." Then, his lips, which had come back to life again.

"Forever," he said slowly. The reality of it all dawning on him. She knew she would need to provide an explanation, that he would need to adjust to this new reality before him. But then he gave her a smile, as if excited for that future together.

He trailed his fingers over his exposed chest. "What does it mean though? Now that I hold this in my chest."

"I don't know." she said honestly. They would need to speak with Sveta to get answers. Perhaps the Weather Gods would be merciful and not punish her too harshly. "I assume you'll be put into danger each year. In the Undertaking." Her new goal would be to find him and make sure she reached him in time. "I hope that's okay."

He smiled back at her, freely and openly. "I'm not scared at all. I trust you."

"I would hope so," she said. "You're now stuck with me."

He leaned his forehead against hers, and she took him in. His scent, his skin, and his breaths that filled her with calmness. She never wanted to exist in a world without him.

His hand slid against the wet ground and they were reminded that this was not over quite yet.

"We should go," she said. She got up carefully and helped him to his feet. They stood there just staring at each other for too long, acting like they had more time than they did. He stepped forward and hugged her, and she melted into him. She would be able to do that everyday now. That truth had her own heart skipping.

He took her hand, and they sprinted off to escape the maze together.

Epilogue

Zimyn sat next to his wife. She wore his mother's ring with pride. The carriage bounced against the uneven road, while Ludelle busily read through some papers on trade deals. He loved watching her lead and attend to her courtly duties, even if it meant spending less time with him. She was a Queen without an advisor now. He couldn't complain, though. Balvan deserved his death. She had made the right choice.

When they stepped out of the Undertaking, many of the court's people waited on the other side, wanting a glimpse of the new couple. There was a uniform gasp that sounded when they saw Ludelle and Zimyn together. Ludelle had a lot of convincing to do, especially with the other nobles. But she did it, with her head held high and not a sliver of hesitation. She had won the Undertaking. She had retrieved the Heart and power was restored for one more year. That's all that mattered. Who laid in her bed was only for her.

She already offered a solution to the issue of having no advisor. Each region of the court would choose a representative that would have a seat on a council. Ludelle hosted them as guests at the castle, and they all spoke to her about any issues they may be experiencing. It kept her busy, but when she came back to their room, Kotyn and Zimyn spoiled her.

They kept the fact that the Heart was inside of him from everyone except Sveta, who seemed to know immediately what had transpired. She had agreed with Ludelle's assessment. Zimyn would now need to risk himself as Ludelle scoured her Undertaking each year to save him. He couldn't be more honored to play such a monumental role.

His father had also learned the truth. He cried, nervous for his only son to be put into danger, but Ludelle reassured him. She would gladly claw her way to her love each year.

Best of all, Zimyn got to attend any official court business across courts with Ludelle as his wife. His scales were gone, and he was happier without the weight of them, even refusing when Ludelle offered to replace them. Flix had been managing as Captain perfectly.

"You're distracted," Ludelle quipped.

Zimyn leaned over, lightly biting her neck. "You're distracting. Especially when you are busy thinking."

"I'm always thinking."

He chuckled against her skin and he could feel the gooseflesh that he caused. Only he could make the Snow Queen shiver with his heat. "That's why you'll be the death of me."

He meant it in jest, but there was a bigger truth there that even Ludelle didn't know. After they spoke with Sveta, she took him aside and informed him that because the Heart was inside him, it would need to be removed once their heir took the throne and began their own Undertakings. He would need to die so that his future child could rule. It was a sacrifice that Zimyn had no qualms with because they had a long while until then, so he would savor each breath he had.

One day, once Ludelle had settled into this new way of ruling, he would tell her. He wasn't scared for when that time came. He didn't want her to have any regrets either. She saved him, she chose him, and that was the greatest gift of all.

Acknowledgements

G iving self-publishing a go was not originally on the docket. I was querying my fairy tale retelling *The Bone Below* and not having too much luck. I sent out one more batch to agents and small presses and promised myself if it didn't work out than I would self-pub that novel. Luckily, I got an offer from the most amazing small press after that, but, the urge to self-pub didn't go away. The only thing was I had nothing else written yet. Then, one day, the idea for The Weather Court Gem series came to me, and I knew this was the perfect set of stories.

I am so grateful for everyone who had a hand in making this a reality. It's truly a daunting and exciting learning experience, and the people by my side made it less overwhelming.

I can't thank Aubrey, my amazing cover artist, enough. She brought my visions to life. I truly can't stop obsessing over these covers. You truly are a gem to work with and are so good at your craft.

Des, my talented editor, gave life to my manuscript. Handing over your words to an editor can be scary, but I trusted Des immediately because I could tell how much she cares for her authors. That's such a privilege, and I am so lucky to have found her. Thank you so much for taking care of my stories.

To anyone who took a chance on this little novella: thank you from the bottom of my heart. I can't wait to share the rest of the stories from this series, and I hope you are excited to join me on this journey.

About the Author

K C Silver is a born and raised Chicagoan, spending her days exploring the city, one train stop at a time. She currently works as a media planner at a large media agency where she daydreams of the day when a Slack notification no longer makes her heart jump in fear.

KC enjoys character driven stories where the main character is on a journey of discovering themselves and learning to let go of the expectations weighing on them, while falling in love.

Of Snow and Sapphire is her first novel under her pen name. She can be found on all socials at @bysilverstories